"You must think I'm an awful mother,"

she said, lifting tearful eyes.

To his surprise, he thought Heller Moore was utterly beguiling, beautiful and brave. "Uh, no. No, it's obvious you're doing the best you can."

She smiled at Jack. "Working two jobs and being a mom to three kids is definitely all I can handle right now. Problem is, I have to try to be a dad, too."

He said it before he thought. "Then maybe your son was right to advertise for a father. I—I mean, that's one thing the boy does understand, that you can't do it by yourself. Otherwise he wouldn't be trying to find you a husband and we wouldn't be here now, would we?"

Heller studied him pointedly for a few moments and said, "I know why I'm here, but I'm not quite certain why you are."

And then he surprised them both by replying, "Maybe I mean to apply for the position."

Dear Reader,

In Arlene James's *Desperately Seeking Daddy*, a harried, single working mom of three feels like Cinderella at the ball when Jack Tyler comes into her life. He wins over her kids, charms her mother and sets straight her grumpy boss. He's the FABULOUS FATHER of her kids' dreams—and the husband of hers!

Although the BUNDLE OF JOY in Amelia Varden's arms is not her natural child, she's loved the baby boy from birth. And now one man has come to claim her son—and her heart—in reader favorite Elizabeth August's *The Rancher and the Baby*.

Won't You Be My Husband? begins Linda Varner's trilogy HOME FOR THE HOLIDAYS, in which a woman ends up engaged to be married after a ten-minute reunion with a bad-boy hunk!

What's a smitten bookkeeper to do when her gorgeous boss asks her to be his bride—even for convenience? Run down the aisle!…in DeAnna Talcott's *The Bachelor and the Bassinet*.

In Pat Montana's *Storybook Bride*, tight-lipped rancher Kody Sanville's been called a half-breed his whole life and doesn't believe in storybook anything. So why can't he stop dreaming of being loved by Becca Covington?

Suzanne McMinn makes her **debut** with *Make Room for Mommy*, in which a single woman with motherhood and marriage on her mind falls for a single dad who isn't at all interested in saying "I do"…or so he thinks!

From classic love stories, to romantic comedies to emotional heart tuggers, Silhouette Romance offers six wonderful new novels each month by six talented authors. I hope you enjoy all six books this month—and every month.

Regards,

Melissa Senate,
Senior Editor

Please address questions and book requests to:
Silhouette Reader Service
U.S.: 3010 Walden Ave., P.O. Box 1325, Buffalo, NY 14269
Canadian: P.O. Box 609, Fort Erie, Ont. L2A 5X3

DESPERATELY SEEKING DADDY

Arlene James

Silhouette

R O M A N C E™

Published by Silhouette Books

America's Publisher of Contemporary Romance

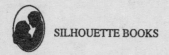

SILHOUETTE BOOKS

ISBN 0-373-19186-3

DESPERATELY SEEKING DADDY

Books by Arlene James

Silhouette Romance

City Girl #141
No Easy Conquest #235
Two of a Kind #253
A Meeting of Hearts #327
An Obvious Virtue #384
Now or Never #404
Reason Enough #421
The Right Moves #446
Strange Bedfellows #471
The Private Garden #495
The Boy Next Door #518
Under a Desert Sky #559
A Delicate Balance #578
The Discerning Heart #614
Dream of a Lifetime #661
Finally Home #687
A Perfect Gentleman #705
Family Man #728
A Man of His Word #770
Tough Guy #806
Gold Digger #830
Palace City Prince #866
*The Perfect Wedding #962
*An Old-Fashioned Love #968
*A Wife Worth Waiting For #974
Mail-Order Brood #1024
*The Rogue Who Came To Stay #1061
*Most Wanted Dad #1144
Desperately Seeking Daddy #1186

*This Side of Heaven

Silhouette Special Edition

A Rumor of Love #664
Husband in the Making #776
With Baby in Mind #869
Child of Her Heart #964

ARLENE JAMES

grew up in Oklahoma and has lived all over the South. In 1976 she married "the most romantic man in the world." The author enjoys traveling with her husband, but writing has always been her chief pastime.

If MR Tyler Married My Mom!

MOM   MR.Tyler   ME   My sister yuk!   My brother

Chapter One

It was as common a sight to Jackson Tyler as his own face in the mirror—a crayon portrait of some small artist's favorite subject on notebook paper. In his five years as a primary and elementary school principal, he had seen thousands of such. What set apart this slightly lopsided rendition was its location. It had been pinned—not upon some lightly scuffed school corridor wall—but at waist height amid the jumble of the large, square, community bulletin board mounted upon the brick facade of the Lake City Grocery. Curious at seeing the familiar in such an unexpected place, Jack shifted the sack of groceries he'd just purchased into a more comfortable position and strolled over for a closer look. Ignoring the protest of his left knee, he crouched down to study this young person's artwork.

Despite the awkward positioning of the drawing in relation to the edges of the paper, it was, without question, a masterpiece, an unusually piquant rendition of, Jack felt certain, a real woman's face, a woman with enormous blue eyes that tilted upward at the outer edges, a rather pointed chin, and a great deal of long, light brown hair with bangs that covered her eyebrows. Interesting. Even given the young artist's above-average expertise, Jack's experienced eye told him he was looking at the work of a child on the underside of nine, a conclusion bolstered by the youngster's deficiency in spelling. Jack first read the left-handed block printing with a chuckle, then sobered as the implications sunk in.

HUSBAN WANTED
FOR PRETTY LADY WITH 3 GOOD CHIDREN
WORKING TO MUCH
NICE
SMART
TIRD
CALL 555-1118
ASK FOR CODY

Some sensitive little person had been moved by a working mother's exhaustion to advertise for aid in the form of a husband. Jack sensed a child in distress and a mother who was going to be very embarrassed.

Oddly disturbed, he took the "ad" from the bulletin board, slipped it into his grocery sack, pushed up to his full, considerable height and walked rapidly across the parking lot to deposit all in the back seat of his sensible, late-model sedan. He hoped for both child's and mother's sakes that no one else had bothered to investigate as closely as he had. He would hate for a child's misguided attempt to help an overwhelmed parent to result in crank calls, derision, or—God forbid—even danger, and he felt himself to be in a unique position to head off disaster. It was, he felt, his duty, if not his responsibility.

After stopping briefly at his apartment to put away the groceries, Jack took the drawing and drove down the street to the sprawling blond brick building set high on a grassy knoll. Some neighborhood children were playing in the sand beneath the vacant swing set, and Jack made a mental note to ask the custodian to rehang the swings. They were always taken down at the end of the school year for routine repair and maintenance, but Jack knew from experience that the custodian would not rehang them until he was told to. Old Henley considered a fully equipped playground an open invitation to aggravation during the summer. Jack considered it a necessary service to a neighborhood lacking a decent city park.

Using his key and alarm code card, he let himself into the empty building and walked blindly down the darkened hall with ease. He knew every square inch of the school building inside and out, not from necessity but from sheer delight. He loved it here. He loved the building, the employees, the teaching, the organizing, even the problems, everything—but especially the children. He always missed them when they were gone, the humming, bubbling, laughing, shouting tumult of two hundred or so little bodies vying for space and attention and knowledge. This early in the summer vacation, the building was almost always empty, but soon the custodial staff would start to ready the building for resuming classes. Later the administrative staff would gradually begin planning and organizing until classroom assignments were again finalized and teachers themselves would return to begin sedately setting up their individual rooms and forming teaching plans. Every available resource would be divvied and balanced and parceled and traded until everyone had what was needed to educate, entertain, engage and otherwise meet the sundry needs of every student. Meanwhile he had the place to himself.

He unlocked the door to his secretary's office, flipped on the overhead lights and booted up the computer that took up the entire side board of her desk. In short order he had pulled up the appropriate cross-referenced file on one Cody Swift Moore, eight years old, recently promoted to the third grade. Before going any further, Jack went to the file cabinet in the corner and looked up the sheet of photos that contained Cody Moore's gap-toothed, grinning visage. Oh, yes. He remembered Cody well as a bright boy in clean, worn clothing, whose hair was sometimes not combed as neatly as usual and whose nose often ran relentlessly. He was one of those children on the cusp, an "at risk" child who somehow had thus far managed to have what he needed to thrive, but just barely.

Returning to the computer, Jack pulled up and printed out Cody Moore's complete file, then carried both the printout and the portrait into his own office for perusal. Turning his chair at an angle, Jack lowered his six-foot-two-inch frame into its welcome embrace, leaned back and propped both feet on the corner of his desk. Idly massaging his left knee, he began to read.

It was just as he had suspected. Cody's parents were divorced. He and a younger sister and a baby brother lived with their mother. No information was given on the father, but the mother's name was listed as Hellen, a possible misspelling of a familiar but uncommon name in this day and time. No home phone number was listed, and the address given was a particular lot in Fairhaven Mobile Home Community. Jack knew it well.

One of the older such communities in the area, it lacked the modern amenities of the newer, tightly controlled parks that had sprung up along the interstate that connected Dallas and Fort Worth with what had once been "the country." There were no swimming pools, meeting halls or game rooms in Fairhaven, no central post boxes, no newspaper kiosks, no picnic grounds, not even paved parking pads, or curbs and gutters for that matter. Yet he had always found the haphazard collection of older mobile homes inviting. Nestled beneath tall, stately shade trees, they were more homey than the fenced, cemented, landscaped, carbon-copy, postage stamp lots with their modern modular homes surrounded by sun decks, car ports, satellite dishes and storage sheds that resembled oversize doll houses.

Fairhaven looked like a place where a kid could play in the dirt with a spoon in some secret, shady bower that belonged to no one and everyone, building dreams and inventing games with easy freedom. It also looked like a place of last chances, where disaster was held off with one hand and survival clutched at with the other. The turnover in rentals was a sometime weekly thing. Odds were even money that the address was no longer valid.

Jack laid aside the papers and groomed his mustache with gentle strokes of his left index finger, thinking. He decided upon his approach, picked up the telephone receiver and punched in the digits written in crayon. A young woman's voice greeted him at the other end of the line.

"Hello. My name is Jackson Tyler. Have I reached the Moore residence?"

"Yes."

"Excellent." He identified himself as the school principal and said that he was trying to update school files, which was perfectly true. "Are you by chance Cody Moore's mother?"

She was not. She was the baby-sitter.

"Could you please tell me, then, how I can contact Mrs. Moore?"

"You mean, like, now?"

"Yes, please, if that's all right."

He was told that he would find Cody's mother at the cashier's counter of the Downtown Convenience Store. "But she don't like to take phone calls down there."

"I see. Well, thank you for being so helpful."

"Sure. Want me to tell her you called?"

He considered. "It's not necessary. I'll get in touch."

He hung up, logged off the computer in the other room and left the building.

Lake City was a small town on one of the most popular lakes in Texas. The recreation areas that serviced the town had been built by the Corps of Engineers. It was a short drive to the corner of Lake Street and Main—a prime location for a convenience store, given its gas pumps, lottery machines and drink coolers. It was without a doubt the busiest place in town, especially during summer.

Jack had to wait while a carload of swimsuited teenagers and a truck towing a pair of jet skis on a trailer got out of his way before he could even turn onto the lot. Vehicles were parked three deep at the curb, many of them linked to various types of water craft. Every gas pump was occupied, and a line had formed in front of the air compressor. Jack left the car well out of the gas pump lanes, locked it and walked across the hot pavement. He held the door open for a trio of women with a number of small children in hand, then slipped inside.

The cashier's station was the hub of the store. It was a square of glass cases, polished chrome and Formica counters staffed by a single individual—a petite woman with a triangular face set with enormous, almond-shaped eyes and framed by a long, lush fall of light ash brown hair. Jack had little doubt that he was looking at Hellen Moore. Cody had captured his mother well—as well as possible with crayons and an untrained hand.

Jack saw at once that she was skilled at juggling half a dozen customers at any given time. Had she not been, she wouldn't have lasted ten minutes in this madhouse. Unfortunately this was neither the place nor the time for the discussion he had in mind. Nevertheless he was in no way deterred. He had come this far, after all. He got into a line of customers and patiently waited his turn, which was more than could be said for some others.

"Hey, move it up there!" yelled a shirtless young man with blond hair straggling about muscular shoulders. He shook his head and flexed his muscles with impatience, his bare feet shifting restlessly as he moved a six-pack of beer from one hand to the other.

"Keep your shorts on, pal," came the smooth rejoinder, "since that's all you're wearing." She'd delivered the line without even looking up, ignoring the chuckles it elicited while punching prices into the cash register with one hand and placing articles into a paper bag with the other. "That'll be six sixty-eight. Out of ten. Six sixty-nine, seventy, seventy-five. Seven. Eight. Nine and ten. Thanks. Come again. Next."

She turned to the line on the other side of the checkout and began punching in a new set of numbers, while the previous customer moved away from the counter and was replaced by a new arrival from the line.

"You got first aid supplies in here?" someone called out from across the room.

"In the corner next to the ice machine," she shouted, then dropped her voice to a more moderate level. "You owe me six cents, ma'am. That's all right, forget the penny. Just remember when you hit that next pothole that the state didn't get their full share. I'll be right with you, sir. Want your candy in a sack, hon? That's one, two, three, four, five at three cents a piece. Exact change. A cashier's angel! Suppose there's a patron saint? Saint Quick Stop, maybe?''

And so it went for a solid quarter hour, nimble fingers flying, answers, comments and wisecracks tossed out with dry humor and quick wit. In the midst of the chaos, she kept her cool, refused to be pushed by those who had nothing more taxing to do than wait their turns and complain about it, and made every movement a study in efficiency.

Jackson found himself watching her with interest and growing pleasure. He liked that wealth of light ash brown hair. It hung almost to her waist, thick and shining, with what, upon closer examination, appeared to be a smattering of individual silver hairs. She wasn't exactly beautiful. Her facial features would never be called classical. Yet to Jack it was an extremely interesting face, with a broad forehead and delicate, pointed chin; thin, tip-tilted nose; and a small but mobile, rose pink mouth. She couldn't stand more than five feet and two or three inches, petite but not really dainty, with small hands and short, almost blunt fingers. Beneath the open, oversize, cotton smock, faded T-shirt and worn blue jeans was a solid, compact body with all the requisite curves—ample curves and in comfortable proportions. Moreover she carried herself with confidence and pride, standing with back straight, shoulders squared, legs spread slightly, as if ready to take on all comers and expecting to walk away a victor. All in all, a very interesting woman. Very interesting.

Business was relentless, but as always she stuck with it, handling several tasks at once, keeping every sense alert and ignoring the physical discomfort of sheer exhaustion. The latter was especially difficult, given that her feet felt as if the soles had been pounded by metal rods, her back ached unrelentingly and her hand was cramping. Worse, she needed to make a visit to the ladies' room, despite having confined her fluid intake for the whole morning to a few sips of badly needed coffee.

She winced inwardly even as she wished a regular customer good luck on the lottery ticket he had just purchased and turned to quirk a brow at the big, good-looking fellow who'd been blatantly staring at her from the moment he'd entered the store. He smiled, holding her gaze, and she barely resisted the urge to thin her lips in a gesture of disdain. The last thing she needed just now was a flirt. She kept her manner brisk.

"What can I do for you?"

He leaned forward slightly as if fearing that she couldn't hear him from that great height. "My name's Jackson Tyler."

As if she cared. With neither the time nor the inclination to chat, she turned her back on him and started ringing up cigarettes, sodas and snacks for three women and a mob of kids.

He cleared his throat and said from behind her, "I'm, uh, the elementary school principal."

"That so?" She counted six sodas at sixty-five and one on sale at forty. Make that two. She jerked her head at one of the mothers. "The little one in back there is about to drop her drink." The little girl screeched like a banshee when her anxious mother rescued it from her too-small hands. No one paid her the least mind. Anyone with experience with a kid that age knew that most of them were banshees.

"The thing is," Jackson Tyler was saying in his deep voice, "I need a moment of your time."

"Don't have a moment," she said over her shoulder, whipping open a sack and dropping packets of cigarettes and candy bars into it. "Is that everything, ladies?" Receiving a nod in the affirmative, she gave the women their total and continued sacking while a whispered conference took place, bills and coins trading back and forth.

"You are Hellen Moore, aren't you?"

He was persistent, she'd give him that. "Hellen? No." She shook out another brown paper bag and began carefully setting cold drinks inside.

"Oh." He sounded disappointed and puzzled. "Well, do you happen to know where I might find her?"

"Couldn't say. Who gets the receipt and the change? Watch the bottom of that bag. Those bottled drinks sweat right through them in no time."

She turned back to the big man, her gaze flicking over him in the seconds that it took those three mothers to start their brood toward the door. She was almost sorry that she couldn't spare the time for a little banter. He looked like a pleasant sort, prosperous, cool and neat in soft tan slacks and a green-and-white-checked shirt with short sleeves and a button-down collar. His straight, golden blond hair had been parted just so, but was too fine and thick not to fall over his forehead. Soft hazel eyes were set beneath straight, thick brows the same bronze brown as the neatly trimmed mustache. He had a full upper lip and balanced features too large for any other face, any face without those brick jaws and that square, jutting chin. Ah well. No help for it.

"I'm kinda busy here," she said bluntly. "Want to move along?"

He flattened enormous hands on the countertop and expelled a breath. "This is important. I was told that I could find Mrs. Moore here."

She folded her arms, wondering if she was going to regret this. "I'm Mrs. Moore."

"Cody's mother?"

She was definitely going to regret this. "That's right."

"Isn't your name Hellen?"

"No."

"No?"

She rolled her eyes. "The name is Heller, all right? *H-E-L-L-E-R*. Now spit it out, bud, or disappear. I'm working here."

"Yeah, she's working here," put in a wise guy from the other side of the counter.

She shot him a deadly look. "Put a clamp on it, youngster, and I'm going to need ID on the beer."

"Uh, I must've left it in my other pants."

"Yeah, right, and I'm a fairy princess, which makes you the toad. Better luck next time, and put it back in the cooler where you got it."

He stomped off in disgust, sixteen if he was a day. She shook her head. Kids.

"Maybe you didn't understand me the first time," the big guy said. "I'm the principal at your son, Cody's, school. Name's Jack Tyler."

For the first time, his urgency touched her. "Something up with Cody? School's out, for pity's sake. What could be wrong?"

He looked distinctly uncomfortable, the tip of one finger stroking his mustache. "Look, I'd rather not discuss it here. What time do you get off work?"

"Late."

"Oh. Well, what time do you start in the morning?"

"Early."

"I could meet you in my office at eight."

Eight. She'd have to leave the house an hour early, lose a whole hour of sleep, leave the kids that much longer. She sighed, dead on her feet already, with eight hours still ahead of her and knowing that she would be aching in every bone come morning. Jack Tyler seemed to take her hesitation as a lack of concern. He put on his principal's face, the one he must use when doling out discipline. She'd have taken issue with that assumption on his part—if she hadn't been busier than a starved cat in an aviary. Cody was her oldest—a good, solemn little boy who sometimes got strange ideas. *Oh, Cody. Cody, honey, what have you done?* No use thinking on it now. She wouldn't know what was up until Jack Tyler chose to tell her, and she didn't believe in borrowing trouble. She had plenty already, thank you. Just living was trouble.

"I must insist on a conference," Tyler stated firmly.

Heller sighed and nodded. "Okay."

"I'll expect you in the morning at eight, then."

"Eight," she confirmed, following him out the door with her eyes even as she smiled at the next person in line. Her son's principal was limping, but it wasn't her problem. "What's this," she quipped, winking at the elderly gentleman who pushed forward a pint of milk and a banana, "moo juice and monkey pod?"

"Health food," the old man replied, a twinkle in his eye. "Dollar fifteen."

He forked over two bucks and gave her a good look at his dentures. "Keep the change."

"Ooh, a true gentleman! Thanks."

The jaunty tone was so practiced that it was second nature, a useful trait for a single mother with too much worry and too little of everything else. She'd buy something sweet for the kids with her extra eighty-five cents, a small treat for Betty to give them with their lunch tomorrow, something to let them know that Mom was thinking of them—a package of cherry licorice whip, maybe, something they wouldn't recognize as a pathetic attempt on her part to give them what other children routinely took for granted.

Her manner was a little softer with the next few customers, her eyes glistening with a brightness that no one watching her would have taken for tears. She couldn't have said herself why she had to beat down the impulse to cry. Maybe it was the combination of a new worry and a small kindness. Maybe it was the unending weariness of working two jobs just to keep body and soul together, and maybe it was the vision of a future that was merely the present all over again, never changing—unless it was for the worse.

Jack gritted his teeth, determined not to look at his watch again. It would only tell him what he already knew. She was late—and getting later by the second. He told himself again that she would definitely show. The subject of this conference was her own son, after all. Of course she would come. He looked at his watch.

Thirty-five minutes! Where the devil was that woman? Sleeping in? Sipping an extra cup of coffee? If she didn't care enough about her boy to expend just this much effort on his behalf, then he was wasting his time trying to help.

It wasn't his problem, anyway. He couldn't force her to listen to him. Fact was, he wasn't even certain what he would have said. Well. So. That was that, then.

He leaned back in his comfortable leather desk chair and expelled a long, cleansing breath. Okay, what now? Might as well do something useful since he was already here. He consulted his calendar, thumbing through the daily pages. The few items on his agenda were either already in the works or simply held no interest for him. Oh, well. He was supposed to be on vacation for the next couple of months, anyway. He'd do something fun, maybe call up some of his old teammates, set up a fishing trip or two, talk about old times. He could even drive down and hang around training camp when that started—except he really didn't want to. He'd lost his enthusiasm for football even before he'd pulverized his knee.

He laid his head back and closed his eyes, waiting for a good idea to come to him. He thought of movies he wanted to see and books he wanted to read and letters he ought to write. Problem was, he didn't want to do any of those things just then. Golf. He'd get out the clubs, rent a cart and make a day of it. All he needed was a partner, someone who could get away on the spur of the moment and hit the links. He picked up the phone and started calling some of the other educators he knew. The three he caught at home, he also woke. He put down the phone with a mutter of disgust, snatched a pencil from the hand-painted cup presented to him at the end of the year by Mrs. Foreman's first-grade class and began bouncing the eraser on the edge of his desk, tapping out words and phrases in Morse code. When he realized that he was tapping out *H-E-L-L-E-R,* he threw the pencil at the trash can. It ricocheted off the rim and flew into the corner, the lead breaking off.

Blast that woman! Didn't she know her kid was hurting for her? Didn't she realize that Cody could see her struggle, that it scared him? He was a little boy who desperately needed some reassurance. Jack pushed his hands over his face, telling himself that it wasn't his job to see that the kid had his fears eased. His job was to educate children, not baby-sit them. But just how well could a worried little boy learn?

Jack bit back an oath, the sound coming out as a choked growl, as he launched himself out of his chair and left his office, slamming the door behind him. No woman, he reflected savagely as he strode out of the building and toward his car, was ever more aptly named than Heller Moore.

The place took about five minutes to find. He sat in his car next to the mailbox, which clung to a leaning metal post and bracket by a single screw, and just looked around for several minutes. The house itself, a mobile home sitting up on cement blocks, was small and sagging and rusty in places, but it had a neat, orderly look about it, a certain aura of "home." The far end sat smack up against the trunk of an old cottonwood tree. A hickory that had been planted too close to a wide side window stood at an odd angle, its upper branches literally lying on top of the structure's metal roof, while its lower ones jutted out over the rickety stoop. The back of the long, narrow lot was a tangle of woody shrubs and withered cedars. Someone had tied bows to one of the bushes with strips of cloth.

Leaving his car parked at the side of the street, Jack got out and walked hesitantly across the yard to climb a trio of steps to the stoop. He paused, combing his mustache with his fingers, then abruptly sent out a fist and rapped on the door. He heard a muffled voice speaking unintelligible words. It sounded as if Heller Moore might have tied one on the night before. He raised his fist and rocked the door repeatedly in its frame. Suddenly the door swung open and a large brunette with long, stringy hair waved a hand at him before disappearing inside.

Jack stuck his head into the dim interior. "Hello?"

"What do you want?"

The croaking voice came from his left. He looked into a small, open kitchen to his right. A round maple table with a scorched spot, four rail-backed chairs and a painted wooden high chair took up almost all the space, leaving a mere path in front of the L-shaped cabinet and stove. The enamel on the sink was chipped, the countertop faded. An empty plastic milk jug and an open sleeve of crackers sat in the middle of the chipped yellow stove. An assortment of cereal boxes were lined up neatly across the top of a small, ancient, olive green refrigerator. Jack stepped inside and turned in the direction of the voice.

The living area was little more than a wide hall. A worn, brown, Early American-style sofa with small, round, ruffled throw pillows sat against the wide window, over which ugly green vinyl drapes had been parted to allow the sunlight into the room. A small coffee table had been pushed up beneath the window on the opposite wall. Upon it rested a small television with rabbit-ear antennae wrapped in strips of tin foil, a can of wildflowers at its side. A brown, oval, braided rug covered most of the pockmarked linoleum. A half-eaten bowl of popcorn had been tipped on its side, spilling fluffy white puffs of popcorn across the clean brown rug. The fake wood paneling on the walls gleamed with fresh polish. The glass in the windows shone crystal clear. A dark, narrow hall led, presumably, to the bedrooms. It wasn't much, but it was somehow welcoming.

The brunette was lying in a heap on the couch, her face turned into a pillow. A thin blue blanket was crumpled at her side. She was wearing pink knit shorts which had long ago lost their shape and a huge T-shirt sporting a cartoon character front and back.

Jack cleared his throat. "I'm looking for Heller Moore."

The brunette rolled over to stare at him. Her face was puffy, her eyes rimmed with smudged mascara. She pushed her lank hair out of her face and said, "She ain't here."

Jack's eyes roamed around the dingy room. "Where is she?"

The brunette sat up and gave a shrug. She looked him over frankly, then smiled. He saw to his surprise that she was considerably younger than he'd assumed. "Who're you?"

The question irritated him. "Seems to me you should have asked that before you opened the door."

She shrugged again, unconcerned, and said, "I don't know where Heller is. She didn't come home last night."

Jack felt the taste of acid in his mouth. Why was he surprised and, yes, disappointed? He shook his head. "You tell her Jackson Tyler was here." He pulled out his wallet and flipped it open. Extracting a card, he laid it on the arm of the sofa. "You tell her to call first chance she gets, either number. Understand?"

The big girl nodded and picked up the card. "You're from the school?" she asked, but Jack ignored her, turning back to the open door as a rusty old behemoth of a car bounced up into the yard and came to a halt.

Heller Moore gathered her things and got out from behind the steering wheel. She leaned against the side of the car for a moment, head back as if absorbing the sunshine, then she straightened and walked around the front end of the car. Jack moved into the doorway and lifted his arms above his head, bracing them against the frame. She was at the foot of the stoop before she looked up. Shock and something else registered in her face.

"You!" she exclaimed.

Jack bared his teeth in a smile. Heller Moore had come home, and he meant to give her a welcome she'd never forget.

Chapter Two

Heller shook her head. She should have known she'd find him here. Well, she admired his dedication. Pity she was too tired to tell him so. With a sigh she climbed the steps and endured his glare until he decided to move out of her doorway. She went inside and carefully draped the clothing she'd worn to the store the day before over the back of the chair at the end of the kitchen table. She looked around the room, acutely aware of how small and shabby it must appear in Jack Tyler's eyes. She grimaced at the sight of the popcorn bowl turned over in the middle of the living room rug.

"Betty!" she scolded disapprovingly as she moved across the floor. She stooped and began cleaning up the mess. "I've asked you time and again to pick up after yourself."

"Sorry," Betty grumbled. "But it just happened. I knocked over the bowl when I got up to let him in."

"Well, you wouldn't have knocked it over if you hadn't left it sitting in the middle of the floor," Heller pointed out. She picked up the bowl and started toward the kitchen with it, only to walk straight into Jack Tyler. She bounced off his chest, one hand clutching the popcorn bowl, the other pushing hair out of her face. "Oops. Sorry." She side-stepped and walked around him. As she carried the bowl into the kitchen, she said over her shoulder, "I'm a walk-ing zombie this morning. My replacement didn't show up, so I had to work a second shift at the nursing home."

"Nursing home?" His voice sounded startlingly deep and resonant in such small quarters.

She turned to look up into his face. My, he was big and undeniably handsome. She suddenly felt rumpled and plain in her faded green uniform. She lifted a hand self-consciously to the back of her neck, then scowled. What was wrong with her? She'd decided long ago to let the world take her at face value. What did she care what anyone thought as long as she knew that she was doing her dead-level best? If she looked like something the cat had dragged in, it was be-cause she'd been up all night working in an effort to sup-port her family. She fixed Jack Tyler with a cold glare. "We can't all be school principals," she informed him tartly. "Some of us have to make do as convenience store clerks and nurse's aides."

To her surprise, his hazel eyes gleamed sympathetically before he looked away. "It must be difficult for you," he said quietly, "working two jobs."

Difficult didn't begin to describe her personal daily grind, but she found herself wanting to reassure him. She shrugged. "I manage."

She heard the slap of bare feet on the bare linoleum of the hallway floor and looked in that direction just as Cody wandered into view. His ash brown hair stuck up at odd angles. His bare chest looked painfully thin, the knobs of his shoulders protruding awkwardly before dwindling into stringy arms. There was a small hole near the elastic waistband of his threadbare briefs. She watched him knuckle the sleep from his eyes and felt a surge of motherly love. His big, hazel gaze wandered the room briefly before settling on her. He smiled, his eyes lazily moving on. Suddenly, recognition flooded his face.

"Mr. Tyler?"

"Hello, Cody."

His mouth dropped open, his eyes growing impossibly large in his small face. He shot a panicked look at his mother. "Am I in trouble?"

Heller hurried across the room to slide an arm about his narrow shoulders. "No, of course not." Yet, she didn't know what Mr. Tyler wanted. She eyed him uneasily. It must be important, for him to visit her twice in less than twenty-four hours, and he *had* said that it involved Cody. She tightened her embrace, as wary in her way as Cody, when Jackson Tyler walked forward and bent at the waist, his big hand reaching out to cover the top of Cody's head.

"Must be a shock to wake up and find the principal in your home," he said, humor softening the tones of his deep voice, "but you don't have a thing to worry about. I just want to talk to your mom about a certain advertisement you drew."

Cody's eyes nearly popped out of his head. "Really? Oh, boy! I knew it'd work!"

"Now don't blow things all out of proportion," Tyler warned gently. "This business isn't nearly as simple as you seem to think."

"What business?" Heller asked, puzzled. "What advertisement? What are you talking about?"

Jack Tyler straightened and slid a glance down at Cody, his thick brows lifting. "Didn't tell her, hmm?"

Cody shook his head. "She's too selfish suffishenly," he said with dead certainty.

Tyler chuckled. "Selfish suffish— Ah. I'll remember that. *Self-sufficient* types can pose problems."

Cody grinned, and Jack Tyler winked conspiratorially. Heller folded her arms and began tapping a toe, too exhausted to exercise her patience. "Will someone please tell me what's going on here?"

"Exactly my intention," Tyler said, glancing around at the small room. He stroked his mustache and seemed to reach a decision. "How does breakfast sound?"

She blinked at him. "Breakfast?"

He nodded. "If you're going to work two jobs and stay up all night, you ought at least to eat properly. I'll have you back within the hour, promise." He made a small gesture in Cody's direction. "And it'll give us a chance to talk—in private."

Heller looked down at Cody's bright, expectant face. He gazed at Jackson Tyler with an oddly covetous expression. What on earth was going on here? Well, there was only one way to find out. She pushed aside the physical exhaustion and met Jackson Tyler's gaze with curiosity.

"Just let me brush my hair and wash my face."

Cody literally jumped into the air, smacking his hands together with glee. "All ri-i-ight!"

Heller placed a restraining hand on his shoulder. "Don't wake your brother and sister."

He ducked his head apologetically, still grinning. "Sorry."

"And get dressed. It's not polite to run around the house in your underwear."

He nodded compliance. She smiled approvingly and tilted his face up for a kiss. He flung his arms around her neck and smacked her noisily on the mouth. She noted that she didn't have to bend as far as she had only a month or so ago. He was growing up, this first-born son of hers, and much too quickly from her perspective. She wondered what had put that sparkle in his usually solemn eyes and what it had to do with Jackson Tyler.

"I'll only be a minute," she promised, her gaze wandering once more to the big man standing in the middle of her small living room. She turned Cody toward the bedroom he shared with his brother and sister and ushered him down the hall, leaving him at the door with a whispered admonishment to be very quiet. He nodded and slipped inside the room.

Heller hurried on down the hallway to the bathroom. Quickly, she tidied herself, her mind whirling with questions. She wished she had time to change clothing, but she knew that would only delay the answers she needed to quell her concerns. Besides, this was a conference, not a date. She only hoped that whatever Jack Tyler had to say would not threaten the sanctity of her family. God knew they were already holding on by a thread.

Jack waited uncomfortably for Heller Moore to return. Taking her to breakfast had been a stroke of genius. Not only could Heller eat a proper meal in a relaxing setting, he could tell her about the advertisement without embarrassing either her or Cody more than necessary. In addition, it might allow him to deal with the situation without disappointing the boy. He'd read the hope and delight in Cody's sleepy eyes when he'd mentioned the advertisement and had known what the boy was thinking. It did Jack's ego no harm to think the kid was pleased with the prospect of him as a stepfather, however unlikely the scenario, and he'd realized how embarrassed the boy would be to learn of his mistake—not to mention his mother's embarrassment at having his foolish scheme revealed in front of another party.

That other party was even then studying him with narrowed, blackened eyes, as if he were a piece of merchandise on a shelf. He curbed his impulse to tell her to mind her own business, and settled for asking a few politely framed questions in the guise of small talk. In short order he learned that she was the baby-sitter, trading her services for a place to sleep on Heller's couch, meals and a little spending money. Obviously she didn't put herself out more than she had to, and she hadn't displayed excellent judgment in letting him in without so much as a glance at his face or a word of explanation.

He was warning her about the dangers of opening the door to a stranger when Heller returned, still wearing the faded uniform but looking a bit revived. He winced inwardly at the scathing words he'd planned for this small, spunky woman who worked two demanding jobs just to keep her family together in this little trailer. Buying her breakfast seemed a mild atonement for jumping to conclusions. He opened the door for her, noting the quirk of her lips as she marked that small courtesy. Was courtesy such a useless commodity in her life then? It seemed so.

She went straight to his car, waiting beside it with a small, wry smile until he opened the door and helped her inside. Thanking him with a nod of her head and that quirk of her lips, she buckled her seat belt. He walked around the car and slid in beside her. His hand fell automatically to the sheet of paper that lay facedown on the seat between them, but she put her head back, closed her eyes and sighed, exhaustion evident in the slump of her shoulders and the slack muscles of her face. He picked up the paper, folded it and slipped it into his shirt pocket. It could wait until she'd eaten.

The local café had already seen its morning rush and was enjoying the lull before the bustle of preparing for the lunch crowd. Jack waved at the middle-aged waitress sipping a cup of coffee at a table near the kitchen door. She smiled and got up, making her way toward the booth into which he and Heller Moore settled. Heller pulled a menu from beneath the napkin dispenser, murmuring, "I'm starved."

"Morning, Jack!"

He smiled at the waitress, another one of those women who worked unbelievably hard for far too little compensation and looked it. How long, he found himself wondering, before Heller's face and hands began to show the kind of wear and tear that this woman's did? He found the thought unpleasant.

"Good morning, Liz. This is Mrs. Moore."

Liz cracked her gum and grinned down at Heller. "Yeah, I know you. You work down at the convenience store, don't you?"

"That's right." Heller returned her smile.

Liz pulled out her pad and pencil, ready to get down to business. "What can I get you?"

Heller studied the menu she'd opened. Jack glanced at Liz. "Coffee and Danish for me."

Heller snapped the menu closed. "Same."

He reached over and flipped the menu open again. "Order a decent breakfast. I've already had one."

She couldn't quite hide her relief and pleasure. "If you insist."

He winked at Liz as Heller went over the choices again.

"Um, I'll have the Belgian waffle and coffee," she decided.

"Bring her an order of sausage links and hash browns with that," he added, feeling positively expansive.

"Oh, it's too much," she protested, but Liz had already received her instructions and was walking away.

"And rush it," Jack called to the retreating waitress. She flipped an acknowledgment with one hand and stabbed her pencil into the jumble of curls atop her head.

"I'm sorry for standing you up this morning," Heller apologized after a moment.

Jack nodded and shrugged. "I understand. Circumstances beyond your control."

"I couldn't call. They don't allow us to make personal calls from the nursing home, especially long-distance ones."

He nodded again and asked a few astute questions about the place where she worked, learning that it was a small, private facility in a neighboring community. She liked the old folks, she said, but it was heavy work. Thankfully, it was only four hours most nights. Four hours after standing on her feet all day at the convenience store, he mused silently. The food arrived in record time. He mentally promised Liz a generous tip as he watched Heller wade in with relish. For a small woman, she could certainly pack it in. Two jobs must require twice the nutrition, Jack mused.

They were enjoying final cups of coffee, the table having been cleared, when he drew the folded paper from his pocket and placed it on the table. "I found this posted on that big bulletin board outside the grocery yesterday," he said without preamble.

She picked it up, unfolded it and stared at what was revealed. He watched her jaw drop and her face turn hot pink. "Good grief!"

He dropped his gaze to his cup. "It's quite a good likeness, actually," he said softly. Then he ratcheted up his gaze. "I'm sure Cody didn't mean to embarrass you."

She covered her face with both hands, pushed her hair back and sighed, staring down at the crayon markings on the paper. "He wants to help. He knows it's difficult, being a single parent. I try not to let him see, but—" Her voice thinned and wobbled. In another moment, tears dripped onto the lined paper.

Jack sat stunned for a moment, his heart turning over in his chest. He hadn't expected her to cry. That was the last thing he'd expected, and he felt helpless to deal with it. To his disgust, the only thing he could think to do was to take her in his arms and promise her that all would be well. But he couldn't do that. He hardly knew the woman. He settled for fishing a paper napkin out of the dispenser and thrusting it at her. She took it, sniffed and dried her cheeks.

"You must think I'm an awful mother," she said directly, lifting tearful eyes.

To his surprise he thought she was utterly beguiling, beautiful and brave. He gave his head an awkward shake, as much to dislodge the thought as to deny hers. "Uh, no. No, it's obvious you're doing the best you can in difficult circumstances. I just thought I ought to try to spare you and Cody as much discomfort over this little incident as I could. He wouldn't realize how dangerous it could be, posting your telephone number publicly, or that you'd feel . . . well . . ."

"*Mortified* ought to about cover it," she said, shredding a corner of the flimsy napkin. After a pause, she went on. "It's the divorce." She laid her hands on the table and moved her head slowly side to side as if trying to find words to explain what she didn't understand herself.

"Cody's father was never much good at providing for us, so it's no surprise that he doesn't pay his child support. But at least he was there with the children when I had to be away from them." She sighed and lifted a hand to her forehead. "Then I'd come in from work exhausted, and he'd want his night out on the town, his good time, and we'd argue, which was all the excuse he needed to storm out and drink up every extra cent I could pull together."

She dropped her hand and smoothed out the napkin, studying it as if it held the secrets to the universe. "It wasn't the drinking or the carousing I couldn't stand," she went on softly. "I didn't *like it,* but I could stand it. What I couldn't abide was the infidelity." Her voice dwindled to a whisper, so that Jack found himself leaning forward to catch every word. "A woman's self-esteem can't take very much of that, you know. But Cody wouldn't understand that. All he knows is that it seemed easier when I wasn't alone, and for the children perhaps it was." She sighed again and closed her eyes. "I don't know."

Jack cleared his throat, uncomfortable with this intimate new knowledge. He'd never understood how any man could cheat on his wife and face himself in the mirror, but to cheat on this woman? That ex of hers must give new meaning to the word *idiot.* On the other hand, what did he really know about it? He pushed a hand over his face, realizing that he wasn't being very logical. He swept a gaze over her and gulped. He was definitely letting appearance—that was to say, *attraction*—sway his judgment. Realizing that he had to say something in response, he grasped the first harmless thing that entered his head.

"D-divorce is difficult for everyone involved." Oh, brilliant. Tell her something she doesn't know. "S-sometimes it's simply the lesser of two evils."

She nodded. "That's true."

He felt a surge of confidence and plunged on. "Cody can't be expected to understand that, though."

She sighed. "I know. It's just..." She agonized for a moment, biting her lip, then blurted, "I couldn't stand being married to someone who used and abused me." She leaned across the table, imploring him to understand. "Carmody took my money and spent it on other women! It didn't matter to him that the children and I did without. To him, life is all about having fun, and I know that attitude too well to believe I could defeat it. I grew up with that attitude. My father worked only so he could afford to party, with no thought for his children and our needs, and that suited my mother just fine so long as she could party with him.

"But I'm not like that, and I don't want my children to be like that. I thought the divorce would be best for all of us, but maybe I just rationalized that to ease my conscience. I wanted the divorce and I got it. And now my children are suffering for it." Her gaze dropped forlornly to the crayon drawing.

Jack impulsively covered her hand with his. She looked up suddenly, tossing her hair back. Her pale blue eyes were wide with shock. He quickly pulled his hand away, his gaze skittering around the booth as he tried to gather his scattered thoughts. "Uh, you...you did what you thought best. N-no doubt you were right. In a situation like that, what other choice was there?"

She spread her hands in a gesture of helplessness. "If only Carmody would pay more attention to the children. If he'd just help out now and again financially..." One slender brow arched in irony. "He didn't do that when we were married. Why would I expect it of him now? Yet my children need their father. I just don't know what the answer is."

"Maybe you just keep doing the best you can," he said.

Her mouth quirked up on one end. "You think I'm doing the best I can, then?"

He blinked, realizing how much he'd revealed by that one less-than-helpful statement, and looked down at his cold cup. "You were thinking of working three jobs maybe?"

She shook her head, smiling at that. "No. Working two jobs and being a mom is definitely all I can handle. Problem is, I have to try to be a dad, too."

He said it before he thought. "Maybe Cody had the right idea, after all." His own words knocked Jack back against his seat. "I—I mean, that's one thing Cody obviously does understand, th-that you can't do it by yourself. Otherwise, he wouldn't be trying to find you a husband, and we wouldn't be here now, would we?"

She cocked her head at that, studied him pointedly for a few moments and said, "I know why I'm here, but I'm not quite certain why you are."

He was careful to think before he replied this time, and he quickly came up with a number of possibilities. He could say, for instance, that his being here was just part and parcel of his job, that he felt a genuine responsibility for the children who attended his school, that he couldn't ignore the wordless plea of a troubled little boy. He could even say it was simple courtesy or curiosity or pure happenstance. Instead, he heard himself saying, "Maybe I mean to apply for the position."

For the longest moment she stared as if frozen. Jack felt the very same way, as if he couldn't move, couldn't speak, couldn't even think. Then slowly the implications of what he'd said crept over him. He didn't know this woman! Was he so lonely, so empty, that he'd let a misspelled ad drawn in crayon decide his destiny? Did he need his own family so desperately that he'd settle for merely being needed himself? A deep, bitter sense of shame engulfed him. He felt his face burn hot and closed his eyes. He would've bitten his tongue off if it had meant being able to unsay those careless words.

Then suddenly she burst out laughing. Jack stared at her, his mouth open, while the sound of her laughter, so bright and cheerful and healing, built and built. It *was* rather funny—absurd, in fact. His mouth wobbled; he brushed his mustache with his fingertips to still it, but the smile broke free, and a chuckle followed it. That chuckle felt so good that he gave himself up to it. When the merriment played out, she wiped her eyes and braced her elbows on the table-top.

"I needed that."

He nodded, feeling sheepish, as an uneasy new aware-ness tightened the lines of her face. He glanced at his watch without paying the time any real attention and slid out of the booth. "I'd better pay the check and get you home."

"Okay. Thanks."

He made short work of it. Within the minute they were in the car again. She laid her head back and closed her eyes. After a bit he noticed that a smile hovered about her lips. He allowed himself to feel a little gush of pleasure at that. He'd embarrassed himself, but if he'd saved her some embar-rassment in the process . . . well, somehow that was enough.

He brought the car to a stop in front of her house, won-dering if he would have to wake her, but she immediately lifted her head and gave him a clear-eyed look.

"I don't know how to thank you."

He glanced away, not wanting her to see how that pleased him. "Unnecessary. I'd have done the same for any of my students."

"I can see that," she said, smiling warmly. She lifted her hand, Cody's folded portrait clutched in it. "I'll try to make him understand that this isn't a solution."

He nodded. "Just remember to thank him for trying to help."

"I will."

She opened the car door and started to get out, but Jack found that he wasn't quite prepared to let it end like this. He caught her hand in his, and when she stopped to look back at him, he gently pried the folded paper from her fist.

"I'd like to keep this, if you don't mind." He grinned. "I have a kind of collection. Kids have such a funny way of viewing this wacky world of ours, you know, and I find it comforting to remind myself of that from time to time."

"You keep it then," she said, and got out of the car.

He resisted the impulse to kill the engine and walk her to her door. It was the gentlemanly thing to do, but not the wisest, perhaps. He wouldn't want to plant false hope, not after all he'd said, first intimating that she might truly need a husband and then blurting that perhaps he would apply for the position! No, far better to just keep his seat.

She closed the door and backed away, bending a little to look at him through the window and fold her hand in a kind of wave. "Bye."

"Goodbye."

He watched her turn and walk across the dusty yard to the stoop. She climbed the steps, opened the door and paused to wave once more before going inside. He slipped the folded crayon drawing into his shirt pocket, then started the car down the street, telling himself it was over. He'd done his duty. It was all anyone could expect of him, all he ought to expect of himself.

But he couldn't help remembering the way Cody's face had lighted up when he'd believed that Mr. Tyler was there to court his mother, or the exhaustion and regret in Heller Moore's eyes when she'd admitted that she couldn't do it all alone. He couldn't help thinking, either, that Cody's conclusion was right, despite his method of trying to solve the problem. She did need someone, someone who would appreciate her strength and determination, her honesty and spunk. Someone who loved and enjoyed kids. Someone who wouldn't cheat.

He shook his head, surprised at himself. Was he honestly contemplating involvement with Heller Moore? What if he did see her again? Would he find that she wasn't the woman he thought her to be? Would disappointment lead to regret? He'd been disappointed before, bitterly so. Perhaps he ought to consider that a lesson learned and let well enough alone. Perhaps he ought to find someone with whom he had more in common. Another educator? Yes, that was the kind of woman in whom he should be interested. A safe, sensible, middle-class lady with her life together and time to consider him and his needs. He'd give the matter some serious thought, he promised himself. Someday.

Heller caught the baby by the ankle and pulled him back into the middle of the bed.

"Sit still, Davy," Cody scolded, shaking a finger at his little brother.

Davy plopped onto his bottom, stuck his tongue out and waggled his head side to side. "Sit, you'se'f!" He fell back, laughing in two-and-a-half-year-old glee.

Cody scowled. "Why don't you go in the other room, Davy? I'm trying to talk to Mama."

At the very suggestion of being parted from his mother, Davy lunged up and threw his arms around her neck from the back, crying out, "No-o-o!"

Heller patted his chubby arms, swaying beneath his weight against her back. "It's all right, honey. Just settle down now so I can talk to your big brother." She stifled a tired sign and smiled down at Cody's pouty face. "Do you understand what I'm trying to say, son? Marriage isn't like a garage sale, Cody. You can't just post notice and take your best offer."

Confusion dulled his hazel eyes. "But, Mama, Mr. Tyler's a real nice man. He don't drink or nothing, 'cause he's always telling us how dangerous it is, and he likes kids. I know he does! Even when you're bad he still rubs you on the head and stuff. He don't even cuss when he's mad!''

Heller didn't know whether to laugh or cry. She shook her head, hoping to shake some new idea into it, but all she could do was repeat what she'd already said. ''Mr. Tyler is a very nice man, Cody, but he would no more marry some woman he met through an advertisement than he would...cuss in front of you children.''

Cody's thin brows drew together. ''I don't see why not, if he likes you.''

Heller rolled her eyes, then clamped down on the impulse to tear at her hair, closing her eyes and pulling in a deep breath instead. Calm again, she smiled. Davy drummed his knees against her spine, turning the smile to a grimace. She pulled him around into her lap and tucked his head beneath her chin. ''There's one thing you haven't taken into consideration, Cody,'' she told him smoothly, ''and that is that I don't want to get married again.''

He cocked his head to one side. ''How come? Don't you like Mr. Tyler?''

Flabbergasted, Heller just stared at him for a moment. Davy slid down her lap, flopped over and eased himself onto the floor, where he promptly began running circles around Cody. She caught him and pointed him toward the door. He ran screaming down the hallway, then turned around and headed back. Heller pulled Cody to her side, an arm draped around his shoulders. ''Cody, honey, it doesn't have anything to do with Mr. Tyler.''

''But don't you like him?''

''Yes, of course I do, but that doesn't mean I want to marry him.''

''How come?''

She searched for the right words. "You have to have a special feeling for the person you want to marry."

"What kind of special feeling?"

"Well, it's kind of like..." She thought suddenly of that moment back at the café when Jack Tyler had covered her hand with his and electricity had shot up her arm, practically knocking her out of her seat. She shook herself, alarmed. Man, she really had to get some sleep! She hugged Cody and said, "I can't explain it, Cody, and I know you were trying to help me when you put up that advertisement, but please, *please* don't do anything like that again. All right?"

He set his mouth glumly, but then nodded.

She kissed the top of his head. "Thank you, sweetheart. I love you so much." She tilted his face up with one fingertip. "You're all I need, son, you and your brother and sister."

He put his arms around her neck and mumbled against her shoulder, "I love you, too, Mom."

"I know you do, and I'm so glad." She ruffled his hair. Davy burst through the door, squealing like a stuck hog, and threw himself against the bed. Heller caught him by the arms before he fell to the floor and bent down low to hug him. "Okay, who wants to take a nap with Mommy?"

Cody snorted with disgust. "Huh! Not me. Davy, you want to take a nap?"

Davy squirmed free of his mother's hold, shaking his head so hard his eyes wobbled.

"Go on then," Heller said, getting up and throwing back the bed covers. "Betty will give you a snack, then I'll make us lunch before I go to work." She crawled into the bed, settled back onto her pillow and tossed the covers over her lower body. "Kiss-kiss."

Cody smacked her, then held up Davy so he could smear his mouth against her cheek. Heller smiled and closed her eyes. Cody tiptoed out, herding Davy ahead of him, and quietly shut the door. Davy yelled fit to raise the dead and ran down the hall.

Heller turned over, already drifting into a badly needed sleep. She tuned out Davy's grab for attention and Cody's troubling questions and the knowledge that she would have to rise again in less than two hours. A picture formed before her closed eyes. Jack Tyler. She saw that silly little grin he'd worn as he'd sat there across the table from her, heard the flip—yet almost serious—way he'd said, "Maybe I mean to apply for the position."

She felt again the lurch of her heart, the spurt of euphoria and then the immediate, crushing, bitter return to reality. For the briefest of moments she had actually believed him, and then the absurdity of it had hit her, and she had laughed at that silly little woman inside of her, that undying romantic, that foolish, hopeful, needy woman who could believe, even for a moment, that a man like Jack Tyler would seriously want to build a life with a woman like her. She had laughed at herself.

She wasn't laughing now. And in her heart of hearts, she knew she never had.

Chapter Three

She was right in the middle of it with Carmody when Jack Tyler opened the door and walked in. Her heart did an immediate swoon, which only served to ratchet up her temper another notch. She jerked her glare back to Carmody and got right in his face, leaning over the counter so far that her toes barely touched the floor.

"You have some nerve, Carmody, waltzing in six months behind on your child support and asking to borrow my car! Are you out of your mind?"

The object of her wrath bobbed on the balls of his feet and slung thick, pale blond hair out of eyes that one moment looked green and the next blue. "You're never gonna give me a break, are you? I'm behind on the child support because I don't have a job!"

"That's funny," she retorted, dropping back onto her heels and folding her arms. "You play almost every night!"

"For drinks, Heller! For drinks! I haven't had a real

paying gig in a year—because I don't have transportation!''

"And you expect *me* to provide you with transportation?''

"Who else am I gonna ask? Besides, it's to your benefit.''

She bulged her eyes. "My benefit? How do you figure that?''

He dug his hands into his pockets, causing his jeans to sag on his lean frame, and ducked his head. It was his why-won't-you-believe-me look. "I'll give you half my pay,'' he promised solemnly.

Anger momentarily gave way to sheer need. God knew an extra buck would come in more than handy around her house. But Carmody's promises were like water under the bridge, gone and forgotten—especially by him—in less time than it took to recite the alphabet. She shook her head. "Half of nothing is nothing, Carmody. Besides, how do you expect me to get around without my car?''

"I'd be glad to give you a ride anywhere you want to go,'' said a deep, familiar voice.

A thrill shot through Heller. She suppressed it ruthlessly, sticking up her chin and glaring at Jack.

He lifted a cold, unopened soft drink, as if justifying his presence, and muttered, "Couldn't help overhearing.''

Carmody danced closer, ready to seize the opportunity. "There you go, sugar. Problem solved.''

"Oh, shut up!'' she snapped, turning her attention back to Jack. Carmody leaned a slim hip against the counter and prepared to observe. Heller ignored him. "You taking me to raise, Tyler?''

He sat the soft drink on the counter and flicked his gaze over her. "You look full grown to me.''

Heller caught her breath, then let it out again slowly, determined not to overreact. From the corner of her eye, she saw Carmody take an agitated step closer to the bigger man, then fall back again. She pursed her lips against a smile. Jack would make two of Carmody, standing easily four inches taller and outweighing him by sixty, maybe seventy, pounds. Carmody's continued proprietary air irritated her, so she leaned into her side of the counter and smiled up at Jack Tyler.

"The thing is, I get off here at nine, and I have to be at the nursing home by nine-thirty, and that gives me just a half hour to change and get there."

"No problem," Jack said lightly, cutting a glance at Carmody.

"There. See?" Carmody grinned, holding up both hands. Then he suddenly lunged over the counter, snatched Heller's purse off the shelf where she kept it and stuck his hand into the side pocket.

"Carmody!" She made a grab for the purse, but Carmody came up with the keys and danced back out of reach. "Damn you, Carmody Moore!"

"You won't regret this!" he called, pretending she had agreed as he scurried toward the door. He shot a look at Jack, then grinned broadly at Heller and pushed through the door. "I'll have the car back by morning, I swear!"

Heller beat a fist on the countertop. "Oooh! That...*man*, that...*worm!*"

"Want me to go after him? I can stop him."

She had no doubt that he would do it or that he was capable, but she couldn't quite believe that he had made the offer. What was it to him if Carmody all but stole her car? He was too good, this man. Too good to be true?

She realized that he was waiting for an answer. "No, I guess not." She shrugged. "There's a chance of getting some money out of him, I'd be foolish to pass it up."

Jack popped the top on the soft drink can and took a swallow. "What does he do?"

"Oh, he thinks he's some kind of musician, guitar mostly, a little drums. He sings some, too, when he can borrow a hat."

"A hat?"

"It's Country music." She made a face. "Supposed to be, anyway."

He chuckled. "So the ex is a sometime C & W musician."

"And a full-time bum."

"Which is why he's the ex."

She wrinkled her nose. "He should've been a 'never was,' but I was stupid at seventeen."

He gulped and abruptly set down the can. "You were *seventeen* when you married him?"

She nodded disgustedly. "Home was hell, and I was in *luv.*" She grimaced. "Anyway, I thought I was."

He lifted both brows and seemed to think about it. "Well, at least you have the kids."

She smiled. "Yeah. I wouldn't take a million dollars for my kids. They're it, you know?"

He canted his head, turning the soft drink can in circles with his fingertips. "I can imagine."

She nodded, and folded her arms across her middle. She didn't know why she said it, but she did. "I was pregnant with Davy when we split. Came home in the middle of the day sick and caught him in *my* bed with some slut he'd picked up in a bar."

He stared, a muscle ticking in his clenched jaw. After a moment he looked away. Then he picked up the soft drink can. "*Bum* is a mild word for a man who would do that."

She nodded, then she shrugged, keeping her eyes averted. "Ah, well. Done and gone. That's how I think of Carmody Moore, done and gone."

"In your car," he muttered wryly.

She had to laugh. "It's your fault, you know. If you hadn't offered me a ride..."

He slugged back the cola and crushed the can in his fist. "I can still go after him."

He was angry, angry at Carmody; she could see it behind his eyes. A kind of brightness burned there, bringing out the yellow spokes in mottled gray and green irises. He was angry for her. Had anyone else ever been angry for her? She shook her head, telling herself that this man would be angry over any injustice, however small, however far removed from him personally.

"I—if he doesn't bring it back by morning, I'll call the cops," she said softly.

"Your choice."

"Yeah. Um, I am going to need that ride."

He waved a hand dismissively, then dug into his pocket, pulled out a dollar bill and slapped it onto the countertop. "No problem."

She pushed the dollar bill back at him. "Hey, if I can't give away a few soft drinks after all these years, well, I may as well quit, huh?"

He tossed the crushed can into the trash container behind the counter and shoved the dollar back into his pocket. "Nine o'clock, right?"

She smiled, trying to ignore the heavy beat of her heart. "Right."

"See you then."

She watched him walk away, noting again the slight limp. His left leg did not seem to bend as easily as the right. She wondered if he had hurt himself playing white knight to some other needy female. Cody was right about him. Jack Tyler was a good man—too good for the likes of her.

He wanted to be on time, but not early. Standing around like a bump on a log while she bantered with customers and tended to chores was not his idea of a comfortable interlude, mainly because he knew he would have to watch her every movement, hear every nuance of expression in her voice, judge every sparkle and flash of her eye. He wouldn't be able to help himself. She fascinated him. That woman was a pillar of strength. Inside that small, shapely body and pretty head was a woman who had survived a sort of humiliation and hardship about which he couldn't even bear thinking. God knew that what Lillian had put him through was bad enough, but it was nothing compared to what Carmody Moore had done to Heller.

Heller. Man, did that name fit or what? That alone ought to send him fast in the other direction. But somehow, without meaning to, he'd found himself drawn to the woman.

He hadn't meant to offer her this ride, hadn't meant even to step into the store where she worked, but he couldn't seem to stop himself. He couldn't shake the idea that she needed him, *him*, not just a man, but him specifically. Foolish notion. But it drove him out of the apartment early, and then he was reduced to driving up and down Main Street until the clock in his dashboard read one minute before the hour. He pulled up in front of the store, parked and got out.

She was standing behind the counter, marking something down on a sheet of paper with a pencil. Another person, a college student by the looks of him, stood behind her, wrapping an apron string around his waist and tying it into a slip knot. He looked up when Jack pushed through the door. His face was freckled, his red hair shorn close to his head.

"Hi!"

Jack nodded, waiting for Heller to acknowledge him. She finished what she was writing, pushed the paper away and finally looked up. She noted his presence with the slight lift of one corner of her mouth and laid down the pencil before glancing at her wrist. She was wearing a cheap watch with a black plastic band. It counted off the last few seconds to nine, then chirped repeatedly. She dropped her hand and smiled at him. "Just give me a minute to change."

He hadn't expected that. "You change here?"

She nodded as she hurried through an opening in the counter and called back over her shoulder, "I don't dare go home to do it. Davy would hang on my neck and scream for an hour."

He followed her toward the back of the store. "Who's Davy?"

She disappeared through a pair of silver swinging doors. "My youngest."

"Ah." He heard the twang of a metal clothes hanger as it bounced against the metal door. She was changing right on the other side of that thin barrier. That knowledge did strange things to various parts of his body. He turned away, glancing back toward the counter in the center of the store. The other clerk was watching him openly. Jack felt like a damned fool, standing there with his hands in his pockets, his ears straining for the slip and hiss of fabric moving over skin even as he told himself not to listen.

"I'd really like to go by the house," she said, sounding as if she stood right next to him, "but the baby's only thirty months. He's still at that clingy stage, you know?"

"Thirty months," he mused. "That's two and a half years. That's a toddler, not a baby."

She pushed through the door wearing familiar pale green cotton pants and the matching pullover uniform top. Her white leather athletic shoes and a clean pair of socks were in her hands. She shoved them all at him. "Hold these, will you?"

He bobbled them, nearly dropped them on the floor. She snatched up the jeans and blouse she had been wearing and carefully draped them over the hanger. Only then did she say, "Yes, he's a toddler, but he's still my baby, probably the last one I'll ever have."

He heard himself asking a much too personal question. "Would you want another?"

She shrugged. "I wouldn't mind, in the right situation."

He would not ask her to define such a situation. It wasn't any of his business. She started toward the front of the store, barefoot and carrying her clothes on the hanger. He hurried after her, her shoes and socks in his hand. She went behind the counter and collected her purse, then moved toward the front door.

"Have a good evening, Jason."

"Yeah, you, too!"

She went out onto the sidewalk and hurried toward his car. He caught up with her in three long strides, inexplicably irritated. "Here. Let me help you." He unlocked the passenger's door, then opened the back one and reached for the hanger. She released it as she sunk down onto the seat.

"My shoes."

He dropped them in her lap, hung the clothes over the back door and hurried around to get in behind the wheel. She turned sideways in her seat, brushing out her long, thick hair, her purse open on her lap, a rubber band clamped between her teeth. Quickly she gathered up her long hair and looped the rubber band around it. Jack started the car. She sat back and fastened her seat belt, then began dusting off her feet and putting on her socks.

"You work too much," he said bluntly.

She smiled to herself. "I work as much as I have to."

"You don't get to see your kids a lot, do you?"

"Not nearly as much as I'd like."

"Pretty tough life," he commented tersely.

"To tell you the truth," she said, "it's better than everything that went before."

That rocked him back. "It could be easier, though," he said after a long moment.

She nodded. "Could be, but isn't." She tied one shoe and reached for the other. "In a few months, though, Davy will grow out of this clingy stage, and I'll be able to stop by the house to check on them without causing a traumatic scene. In a few more years Davy will start school, and I won't have to spend half my check every week on full-time child care."

In a few months, he thought, *in a few years. And such small consolations to look forward to.* His hands tightened on the wheel.

"I could stop by and check on them if you like," he said offhandedly.

She looked almost amused. "Why would you want to do that?"

For the life of him, he couldn't have answered that. Finally he said, "Thought it might give you some peace of mind."

She fluffed her bangs with her fingertips, watching him. "You've done more than enough already," she said softly.

He shrugged, and they left it at that as he backed out the car and started it down the road. They pulled up in front of the nursing home a quarter hour later.

"What time do I pick you up?"

She just smiled. "No need. I've arranged another ride."

He was surprised to find himself disappointed. "You didn't have to do that."

"Parkinson owes me. I filled in for her the other night."

"Ah." He reached for the door handle, but she stopped him with a hand on his forearm.

"Keep your seat. I can manage." She promptly got out, retrieved her clothing from the back seat and bent to look at him through the opened door. "Thanks—again."

Jack waved a hand negligently. Just then the door of the nursing home opened and a frail old man came tottering out onto the sidewalk. He waved a gnarled hand. "Heller! Heller!"

She looked his way, then flashed a smile at Jack. "Bye!" She straightened and closed the door, hurrying forward to throw an arm around the old man's stooped shoulders. He peered up at her adoringly through thick bifocal lenses. She turned him deftly and steered him back toward the building, listening intently to his animated chatter.

All that strength, Jack thought, *and compassion to spare. Yeah, one hell of a woman.* He watched until she disappeared into the building, the old man still bending her ear with some story or bit of news. He was smiling when he put the car in motion, and he knew exactly where he was going next.

Heller jiggled the key in the lock, alternately pulling and pushing on the doorknob until the ancient mechanism moved into place and the lock released. She waved at the street, signaling to her ride, and opened the door. The television, which sat beneath the window in the wall opposite the door, was the first thing she noticed. It was on, but the sound had been turned down so low that the hum of the air conditioner in the right lower corner of the window had effectively drowned it out. That was odd. Not Betty's style at all. Much too considerate.

Heller shook her head, dismissing the thought. She draped her clothing over the chair that sat at the end of the kitchen table, dropped her purse on the seat and moved across the room to the television. It was as she bent to reach for the power switch that she saw the reflection in the darkened window.

Not Betty. Much larger than Betty. Male. One foot hanging off the end of her couch, the other crammed into the corner, bending the leg at an awkward angle. Her heart in her throat, she skimmed her gaze up his body. He moved, sighing and rolling up onto his shoulder. She whirled around and looked straight into the sleeping face of Jackson Tyler.

For a long moment she could do nothing but stare, her mouth ajar. His hair had fallen forward over one eyebrow, lending him a boyish air, despite the darker mustache and the shadow of a beard. The television forgotten, she crept forward and reached out a hand as if to touch him and satisfy herself that he was real and there on her living room sofa. Suddenly, he sucked in a deep breath, flung an arm up over his head and opened his eyes. He blinked and smiled. "Hi."

She plopped down in the middle of the floor and stared at him. "What are you doing here?"

He rubbed a hand over his face, cleared his throat and pushed up onto one elbow. "What time is it?"

She had to make herself think. "Uh, nearly two."

He nodded as if that explained everything and yawned. "Sorry. Guess I fell asleep."

"Where is Betty?" she asked more sharply than she had intended.

He folded an arm behind his head and looked at her. "I let her leave."

"You let her leave," she repeated blankly, and then she closed her eyes. She was too tired to deal with this, whatever it was, and she couldn't begin to imagine what.

Jack said, "I didn't have anything better to do, so I dropped by to check on things, you know, like we talked about, and when I got here, she was on the phone with a friend. Anyway, turns out her friend's husband has walked out or something, and she was in crisis. So Betty asked if I could stay with the kids for a while, and I figured, why not? So I told her to go."

"Boy, what a chump," Heller teased. "If Betty's friend is who I think it is, she and her husband split up every other week. It's like this game they play." She grinned. "But it was sweet of you to let her go."

He smiled sheepishly. Heller laughed, then abruptly swallowed the sound. "Me and my big mouth!" she whispered. "I'll be lucky if I didn't wake all three of them."

"I think they're sound asleep," he told her. "I just stuck my head inside the room earlier—didn't want them to wake up and see some strange man standing over them—but they were all sleeping like little angels."

Heller rolled her eyes. "Trust me, angels they are not."

"Well, they look like angels," Jack said, struggling into a sitting position, "especially Davy with all that curly hair, and the little girl." He grimaced as he swung his legs off the couch, both hands going to his left knee.

Heller watched the muscles bunch in his jaw as he gritted his teeth and forgot about everything else. "What's wrong?"

"It's nothing," he said through his teeth, "just this stupid knee."

"Nothing?" She moved forward, kneeling at his feet. Sweat popped out on his forehead, despite the fact that the air conditioner was blowing full blast right into his face. "You're in pain."

"My own fault," he said, gritting his teeth. "I know better than to fall asleep on the couch. I always wind up in the wrong position, then the darn thing swells, and I spend the next two days eating aspirin and wearing ice packs."

"Aspirin and ice pack," she mumbled. "I can do that."

She popped up and headed to the kitchen. He tried to wave her back with an uplifted hand. "Oh, hey, no. You don't have to do that."

She ignored him until he started trying to get up, at which point she whirled, pointed a finger at him and, with surprising fierceness, hissed, "Sit down right this minute!"

He gave her a surprised look and collapsed back onto the sofá. She began gathering ice cubes by the flickering light of the television and wrapping them in a tea towel. Then she took aspirin from the cabinet, filled a glass with water and carried everything back into the living room. Settling down on the floor in front of him again, she handed him the makeshift ice pack. He placed it gingerly on his knee. She took the top off the aspirin bottle and held it out to him. He opened one hand, and she shook tablets into it. He promptly slapped them into his mouth, tilted his head back and swallowed. She offered him the water, watching until he'd drained the glass. Then she leaned back on her elbows and gazed up at him.

"How'd you do that?"

"Hurt my knee? Playing football."

"You played in college?"

He nodded. "Yep, then went into the pros."

She lifted her eyebrows, pulling a face. "Really?"

He smirked. "Don't be too impressed. I never made it onto the field, not even to sit on the bench."

"What happened?"

"Nothing too unusual. I reported to training camp, like every other rookie, determined to prove my worth. Then during one of the scrimmages, I twisted a leg and took a hit at the same time. Popped my kneecap, busted bones, tore ligaments."

"Bad, hmm?"

"I sure didn't get up and walk away."

She canted her head to one side. "What happened after that?"

He shrugged. "I went to the hospital for surgery and rehab. The team invoked a cancellation clause in my contract, paid my hospital bills and let me keep the signing bonus, such as it was, and that was that."

End of a dream, she thought, *just like that.* She kept her face impassive, however, sensing that he would not welcome overt sympathy. "That must have been tough," she said.

He shook his head. "Nah, the tough part came later."

"How so?"

He cocked his head, looking down at her, as if trying to decide how much to tell. She knew when he decided to play it conservatively because his gaze skittered away. "You know how it is. Everybody's expecting big things from you, and suddenly it's obvious that those expectations are never going to be fulfilled."

She considered that a moment and softly said, "I guess that shoe was always on my other foot. Seems like I was always the one with expectations."

"In what way?"

She met his gaze evenly. Why not? She had nothing to hide. "Oh, for instance, I expected that marrying Carmody and having my own place would mean I'd have some say about what went on there."

"But it didn't?"

It was her turn to smirk. "Would my husband have brought his women home with him if I had?"

"Guess not."

She shrugged. "Live and learn."

He nodded. "Oh, yeah. Guess we all feel that way."

The feeling of commonality lasted only as long as it took her to look around at her surroundings. "Speaking of expectations," she said, just in case he was laboring under any false assumptions, "I really expected to finish high school and go on to college. Carmody even promised me that I could, but like all the rest of Carmody's promises, he forgot it the minute after he said it. First, he wanted me to just lay out a semester, you know, spend that time with him. Then he had a chance to go on tour, but it meant I'd have to work for a little while. Then Cody came, and that was that."

"It's not too late, you know, Heller," he said carefully. "You can get a G.E.D. and go on to college."

She sighed. "Yeah, it sounds good, but..." She shrugged. "Actually, I got the G.E.D., but I don't have the time, energy or money for college. Probably couldn't get in, anyway."

"Sure you could."

"Doesn't matter, though, does it?"

He said nothing to that, just sat there with her tea towel balanced on his knee. She looked at him, trying to gauge how he was feeling. "How's that knee?"

"Better. Thanks."

"No reason to be thanking me," she said, getting up off the floor. "I'm the rescuee here. You're the rescuer."

He chuckled. "Think so?"

"Seems obvious to me." She reached out a hand. "Let's get you up and out of here. You've done your good deed for the day. In fact, I suspect you've passed your quota for the month. You can go home now.''

He closed his big hand around hers, his gaze direct and steady. ''Maybe I don't want to go home just yet.''

She skewed her gaze around skeptically. ''It's late, hero, and you need to put that knee to bed.''

He had the oddest look on his face, as if he was seeing something that wasn't there, something that surprised and worried and intrigued him all at the same time. Before she could guess what it was about, he tugged on her hand. She stumbled forward and fell against him. He wrapped an arm around her waist and pulled her down onto his lap. The next instant his mouth was on hers, his hand coming up to clasp the back of her neck, his arm bracing her back.

She was too stunned at first to make any response. Then his mouth softened, widened and pivoted against hers. His mustache brushed her skin, both soft and prickly. Electricity shot through her. Her breath retreated, seizing in her chest. Her eyes closed. Feeling blossomed in her breasts, swelling and hardening them. She melted. She had no defense against it.

He let go of her hand and brought his other arm around her, pulling her against his chest. She felt the thud of his heart, and her own answered it. His hands slid over her, warming, kneading, moving upward to cup her face and tilt her head, fitting her mouth more perfectly to his. His thumbs pressed lightly into the hollows of her cheeks, and she instinctively opened her mouth to him. He clasped an arm around her and pushed her head down onto his shoulder, moaning as he thrust his tongue into her mouth, his hand splayed against the side of her head.

She felt that thrust all the way to her toes. She shoved her arms around his neck and sucked his tongue deeper into her mouth, absolutely mindless, excited beyond endurance. She could feel him in places he had never even touched, could imagine his heaviness filling her, pushing her down, enveloping her. His hand slid down her neck and across her chest to her breast. She convulsed, pressing herself against his palm, her lungs working like bellows now.

"Ma-ma!"

Davy's shriek pierced the cocoon of desire and sensation they had spun about themselves. Clarity flooded Heller's mind. Dear God! What was she doing? She fairly leapt off Jack's lap, gaping at him, her body in turmoil. He looked as stunned and shaken as she felt. Davy screeched and collapsed into a bawling heap at her feet.

"Davy!" She stooped and caught him beneath the arms, hauling him up and onto her hip. "You climbed out of your crib again. I'm lowering the bed tomorrow so you can't get over the rail. Don't cry, sweetie. Mommy's here. Hush now. That's it, sweet boy."

He stuck his fingers into his mouth, laid his head against her shoulder and snuffled, looking accusingly at Jack. Jack picked the ice pack up off the floor, where it had fallen, and placed it on the couch, then got to his feet, obviously favoring his left leg.

"I'd better go."

She nodded and bounced Davy on her hip. She couldn't have looked Jack in the eye if her life had depended on it. He limped to the door, opened it and ducked his head, but then he looked back over his shoulder. His gaze went directly to her mouth, then widened to encompass her face. She couldn't tell what he was thinking, wasn't sure she wanted to know, but he was breathing as hard as she was. He went out the door, closing it behind him.

Her legs immediately began to shake. She plopped down onto the couch and fell back against the cushions. Merciful heavens!

Davy began to cry again. She cuddled him and crooned until he hushed and relaxed and faded off to sleep. She kicked off her shoes and stretched out next to him, but she knew she wasn't going to sleep, not for a while. Shock was holding exhaustion at bay, shock and something brand-new. The only term she could find to describe what she was feeling was feminine excitement.

A man she admired had let her know that he found her attractive. She'd almost forgotten what that felt like, if she'd ever actually known, and she was grateful to have been reminded. Yet, as the shock wore off, she found herself fearing this excitement. Jack Tyler was as far above her as the moon. He was an educated man, a former pro football player. It was obvious just by looking at him that he was way out of her league, from the clothes that he wore, to the preppy cut of his hair. They were just too different. She mustn't forget that. Whatever happened, she must not forget that.

Chapter Four

Jack adjusted himself more comfortably in the recliner, a rolled towel elevating his swollen knee, and settled back to enjoy a little daytime television. He had wrapped ice packs around his knee and swallowed the requisite number of analgesics and prescription anti-inflammatory drugs. But he knew from long experience that the most necessary element in reducing the swelling and accompanying pain was time. Thankfully it was summer, and he could afford to wait it out.

During the school year he would be reduced to hobbling around on crutches and sleeping with ice packs on sheets wet from the condensation, and recovery would take twice as long. But there would always be another episode unless or until he submitted to having the joint replaced. He knew the time was coming when he would have to do just that. He'd only resisted this long because he hadn't felt he'd had the time to devote to surgery and recovery. He knew now how hollow that excuse was.

What, he couldn't help wondering, if he were in Heller's position? He didn't even want to think about it. Thinking about it made him feel guilty somehow. It made him want to get up out of his chair and head over to her place, helping out any way he could. And that was the problem. He didn't have any business making himself a regular player over there. If he just hadn't kissed her, he might have been able to help out now and again without getting in too deep, but the damage had been done. He knew that if he went back to Heller's now, it wouldn't be because one of his students needed guidance. It would be personal, very personal, between him and Heller Moore.

And Heller Moore just wasn't what he figured he ought to be looking for.

No matter how he looked at it, that woman and her family were trouble, *big* trouble. He'd have to be mad to take on a woman with her experience and background. Any man to come after Carmody Moore was going to have to pay a price for that bum's maltreatment of the lady. How could she possibly help suspecting every innocent slip of the tongue, every sideways glance, every unforeseen delay? What woman so betrayed and so abused could trust a man again?

Then there was Carmody himself. So untrustworthy a man could not be expected to behave appropriately, which meant that any man involved with Heller Moore would have to accept Carmody as a constant irritant. He was father, after all, to her children, all three of them, and as such could be considered to exert some influence on them, however small. Not a promising prospect for a new man on the scene, no matter how much he might want to help. It was true that they needed help, but God knew it was more than one man could manage alone without devoting himself wholeheartedly to the task.

No, getting involved with Heller Moore was just not a wise move, however much he admired her spirit and dedication and despite the strong physical attraction. He had done what he considered his duty by Cody. Now it was time to pull back. If he'd had an ounce of sense, he wouldn't have gone into the store that day, let alone offer her a ride, then check on her children and wind up baby-sitting. And that kiss.

He groaned aloud just at the memory of it. Nothing could have prepared him for what had happened the instant he'd touched his lips to hers. He wasn't certain even now where it might have led if that little banshee hadn't interrupted them. Good grief, to be saved from one's self by a screaming two-year-old! No, he shouldn't go back there. And since he'd always prided himself on being a reasonable, sensible man with a strong sense of duty and a genuine calling to his vocation, he wouldn't. Except that he did.

He didn't mean to. All the time the swelling was going down in his knee, he congratulated himself on making such a sensible decision. Yet he couldn't help wondering how Heller was holding up. What was going on with her? Were the kids well? He even wanted to know if Betty's friend had patched up her marriage, silly as that seemed. He sometimes found his attention wandering from the game shows, old movies and endless talk shows to some memory of something Heller had said or done or how she had looked at a particular moment, and his dreams were filled with replays of that kiss and imaginative scenarios of what might have happened if Davy hadn't screamed bloody murder. Still, he told himself that he was going to stay away—right up to the moment he turned his sedan into the trailer park.

His timing was excellent. It happened to be Heller's day off. Her old car was parked in the front yard. He could hear the baby screaming from the street, even over the chaotic din of a childish argument.

"I did not!"

"Did, too!"

"So what if I did? You're a mean, stingy, old snot nose, and I hate you!"

"Do not! We're not allowed to hate—"

"Do, too!"

"I'm telling! Mom?"

"Snitch! Tattletale! Rat fink!"

"Shut up!"

"Make me, snot-nose-rat-fink-yellow-belly!"

Jack recognized all too well the signs of an argument about to become a brawl. Without even thinking, he pounded up the steps, opened the door and strode in. Cody and a small, blond six-year-old virago were clawing and pummeling and rolling in a flurry of arms and legs on the edge of the couch, while Davy stood to one side screaming like he'd had his leg cut off without aid of anesthesia. Heller was coming at them from the end of the hallway, her face pale, eyes wide, but Jack got to them first. He got a hand-ful of shirt on each one and pulled them apart, his deep voice booming, "Enough!"

Cody and the girl went instantly limp. Their mouths ajar, heads tilted back, they stared up at him like Aladdin seeing the genie for the first time. In that same instant Heller swooped down on Davy, scooped him up and stumbled with him across the room to collapse upon a dining chair, the toddler sniffing and huffing in her lap.

"That's better," Jack said to the two contestants, but his concern was already centered on Heller. He pushed Cody down on one end of the couch and lifted the girl, who was doubtlessly Cody's younger sister, onto the opposite end. He shook a finger in their faces. "I'll deal with you in a minute, and I don't want to hear another sound out of either of you until then.''

Cody dropped his gaze shamefully, but his sister just leaned back and folded her arms, driving daggers into Jack with her mother's blue eyes. Another hellion. He found himself liking her on the spot, though the emotion was anything but mutual. He turned his back on her baleful glare and walked over to the small dinette table where Heller rested her head in her hands, Davy glued to her midsection like paint on a wall. The table was littered with breakfast dishes. Jack pulled out the chair next to her and sat down.

"Heller?"

She lifted her head with great effort, and her mouth curled into that crooked, wry little smile of hers. He saw the pain in her eyes, recognized it instantly and guessed its source.

"Headache?"

She gritted her teeth and attempted a nod, but finding that simple gesture too painful, she swallowed and whispered, "Splitting."

Davy sighed and rubbed his face against her breasts, drying his tears. Jack got up and went to the cabinet from which he had seen her remove the aspirin bottle. He heard a hiss of protest behind him and turned to find that Heller's daughter had angled her body and was pressing a toe against her brother's thigh. "That's quite enough, young lady," Jack admonished in his best principal's voice. She jerked her foot back and glared murderously at him. Jack took down the aspirin bottle and a drinking glass, which he filled with water and carried to the table.

"Let's get these down you," he said, "and then I'll make some coffee. Caffeine might help."

She gulped down the aspirin obediently, and he busied himself making coffee for the two of them. When it was brewing, he walked back into the living room and stared down at the two children pouting there. After a moment Cody opened his mouth to make his case.

"She drank my chocolate milk!"

"You got more than me, greedy guts!"

"I'm bigger!"

"So—"

Jack shut them up by bending and placing a big hand flat on each narrow chest. "I don't care who did what," he told them sternly. "Your mother has a headache, and all this arguing is making it worse." Both shot guilty glances in her direction, but Jack didn't cut them any slack. "The least you could do is take the argument outside, but I warn you—if it deteriorates into blows again, I'll have to intervene again, and I won't be happy about it. Am I making myself clear?"

Both nodded glumly. Jack straightened. "Fine. Now let this be the end of it."

Cody nodded, but the only conciliatory gesture his sister was willing to make was simply to turn her head away from both him and Jack. At least she couldn't kill him with her eyes that way, Jack told himself as he moved back to Heller's side.

"Show me where it hurts."

"What are you," she croaked, "my guardian angel?"

"Could be." He slid his hands into her hair, massaging her scalp with his fingertips. When he worked his way down to the nape of her neck, she put her head back and sighed. "That's it." He rotated his thumbs against the tendons, applying pressure to the blood vessels beneath the skin.

Heller dropped her head back into his hands and closed her eyes. "Ahhhh."

"This is a tension headache," he said evenly. "The blood vessels are distended. Cutting down the blood flow will lessen the throbbing."

"Ummm," she said. Davy stuck his fingers in his mouth and gazed up at him with big eyes, safe in his mother's lap.

Jack kept up the pressure until the coffeepot stopped sputtering. Then he went to pour two cups and carry them over to the table. Meanwhile, the two on the couch had forgotten their quarrel and occupied themselves otherwise, Cody with a comic book he'd picked up off the floor. The girl was on her knees on the couch, staring out the window and making kissing sounds to a bird on the tree limb just outside. Davy got down off his mother's lap and toddled over to lean against Cody, who eyed him suspiciously and demanded to know if he wanted to go potty. Jack realized then that the child was wearing training pants. An improvement, he decided, and proof that Heller wasn't trying to keep him a baby.

He sat down next to Heller, but kept a wary eye out for trouble from the bubble gum section. "Feeling better?"

She nodded. "Yeah, it's letting up. Thanks."

"Just returning the favor," he said, sipping his coffee.

She did likewise, then said, "How is your knee?"

"Fine. Fine as it's ever going to be."

She looked at him over her cup, her gaze level and open. It occurred to him that she hadn't been the least bit surprised to find him in her living room again. "Can't they do anything about it?" she asked.

He nodded. "They can replace it."

"When you decide to let them," she deduced correctly. "Why haven't you?"

He shrugged. "Well, it's not foolproof. I could wind up with one leg shorter than the other."

"So you'd limp?"

He nodded.

"You limp, anyway," she pointed out pragmatically. "The only difference would be that it wouldn't hurt."

He chuckled. "True, but it takes some recovery time—"

"Oh, and you're so busy saving the world you just can't spare a few days to fix your leg."

He opened his mouth to refute that, then shut it again. What was the use? She would see through any excuse he made. Finally he said, only partly teasing, "It's part of the tough guy persona."

"Tough guy with a heart like melted butter. That stuff might work on the football field, Tyler, but I doubt it pertains to elementary education."

"Hey," he said, "those kids will eat you alive if you show them the slightest weakness."

"Who said a soft heart was a weakness? I happen to respect a guy with genuine concern for the other fellow. And I'll tell you something—they're too few and far between."

He couldn't stop a grin from breaking out. "Is that so?"

"Take it from someone who knows."

He had a snappy comeback perched on the tip of his tongue, but he'd been watching from the corner of his eye as Davy stooped and fished under the couch with one chubby hand, coming up with a fat dust bunny, which was naturally headed for his mouth. "Don't eat that!" Jack barked instinctively.

Everybody in the room froze except Heller, who turned in her seat to see what was going on. Little Davy jerked to a halt, dust bunny poised above an opened mouth. A heartbeat later he wet his pants, pee streaming down his legs and spattering over the floor. He was screaming before it puddled at his feet, the pouf of dust crushed in grimy little fingers. Chaos erupted once more, with Cody and the girl both scolding loudly. Heller took one look at Jack's face and put

her head back and howled with laughter. He felt lower than
a snake's belly, scaring the kid like that, and it didn't help
that Heller was having a good laugh at his expense—again.

"Tyler," she gasped between gales, "you're great at most
things, but potty training isn't one of them!"

"I didn't know he'd do that," he grumbled. "He was
going to eat dirt!"

She got up, still chortling. "Well, now he can make mud
pies. I suppose it's my fault because I haven't checked to be
sure Betty is doing the dusting, not that I have much chance
to. Come on, screamer. Let's get you changed." She picked
up Davy by the armpits and carried him down the hall.

Jack got up and grabbed a roll of paper towels from the
top of the refrigerator. Ignoring the girl's accusatory glare,
he tore off towels and dropped them over the mess on the
floor, prodding them with the toe of his shoe to make certain they soaked up everything. At least the kid hadn't been
standing on the braided rug. When he had the floor wiped
up, he looked around for additional cleaning supplies,
coming up with an appropriate liquid, but he had to go back
to the kids for help after that.

"Where do you keep the mop?" he asked the pair of
them.

The girl slid off the couch and pattered a wide path
around the wet spot on the floor to the kitchen. She stuck
her arm into the dark, narrow space between the refrigerator and the wall and came out first with a broom and then a
mop. Next she opened the cabinet door under the sink and
removed a pail, which she put in the sink. She plunked
the mop head into the sink, hopped up onto the edge of the
counter and turned on the water. Jack walked over to the
sink and reached around her for the handle of the pail. She
slung an elbow, making him back up, and hopped down
again, turning on him with a purely venomous face.

"I'll do it myself! You got no right to! It was your fault, anyhow!"

"All the more reason I should clean it up," he said flatly. He stepped up to the sink, turned off the water, squeezed a small amount of detergent into the pail and carried the whole into the living room, fully aware of the baleful glare drilling into his back.

She followed him back into the living area, silent and reproachful while he wrung out the mop. When he lowered the mop head and began to swab, she lurched forward and grabbed hold of the handle. "I can do it!"

"Punk!" her brother scolded. "Behave."

Jack waved him into silence and released the mop handle. "Fine," he said, backing away. "Have it."

She awkwardly pushed and pulled the mop around in front of the couch, then stopped to sling pale blond hair out of her face.

"Finished?" Jack inquired.

She nodded curtly.

He took the mop out of her hands, nudged her out of the way and swabbed beneath the couch, angling both the mop and his body to get back into the corners. The girl instantly reacted.

"Stop that! You got no right! What are you comin' around here for, anyway? Nobody wants you to!"

"Punk, that's enough!" Heller's voice cracked like a whip, silencing the girl and bringing everything in the room to a halt.

Stopped in the act of sliding off the couch, Cody's eyes were big with misery, moving Jack to lay his big hand comfortingly on the top of the boy's head. Cody smiled up at him gratefully. Jack could hear "Punk" grinding her teeth.

Heller put her hands to her hips and looked down at her daughter. "You owe Mr. Tyler an apology. He was just trying to help."

"But, Mom, it was his fault! He made Davy do it."

"She's right, Heller. I shouldn't have shouted—"

To his surprise she pointed a finger in his face. "You keep quiet. This is my ill-mannered daughter here, and I will deal with her."

He had to bite his lips to keep from grinning. "Yes, ma'am."

She turned her attention back to Punk. "That chip on your shoulder is growing, young lady, and I'm sick of it. When you start abusing guests in our home, you've gone too far, and I won't stand for it. Do you hear?"

To Jack's consternation, the girl's blue eyes, so like her mother's, filled with tears. "He doesn't belong here," she said thickly.

"He's a guest, Punk, and a welcome one. Now you mind your manners, or I'm taking a belt to your behind."

Jack felt miserable. "Heller, could we talk this over, please?"

"Will you let me handle this?" she snapped, a hand going to her head, which he knew was bound to be pounding again.

Jack leaned on the mop and hung his head, wishing he'd kept his big mouth shut from the moment Davy had come up with that dust bunny. How much harm could a mouthful of dirt do a kid, anyway?

Heller was talking loudly and sternly to Punk, who was openly sobbing now. "I want to hear an apology, young lady, and I want to hear it right now!"

Punk sobbed as only a six-year-old with lots of practice can. "Wah-ha-ha-ha!"

Jack shook his head. Cody wrung his hands, saying, "Punk, don't cry. Don't cry!"

Over it all, Heller was saying, "Now, Punk! Apologize now!"

As if that weren't enough, the door opened and none other than Carmody Moore walked in. "What the hell's going on?"

Heller whirled around. Punk flew at him, throwing her arms around his legs and crying, "Daddy! Daddy!"

Carmody's eyes slid over Jack and Heller. "Are you giving her a hard time again?" he demanded of Heller.

"You don't know anything about it, Carmody," she told him, "and I'll thank you not to butt in."

"Butt in? This is my kid here, Heller, in case you've forgotten. They're all my kids."

Heller rolled her eyes, pressing the back of her head with both hands. "What do you want, Carmody?"

His eyes slid over Jack again. "Can't I just stop over to see my kids?"

"Yeah, right," Heller retorted. "If you're after my car again, just forget it. I haven't seen a cent from the last time I loaned it to you, and you promised—"

"Is money all you think about?"

Heller dropped both hands. "I'm in no mood to listen to this. Go away, Carmody!"

"The hell I will. I want to know what's going on here. Why's Punk crying?"

Heller put both hands to her head again, as if to hold it on. "I'm not up to this. I'm not feeling well," she said deliberately. "Please just go."

Jack, who felt perfectly superfluous, was gripping the mop handle so hard that he was in danger of leaving fingerprints in the brittle wood. Carmody sneered at him, then at Heller. "What's the matter, sugar? Morning sickness got you again?" He turned the sneer back to Jack. "You want to be real careful, hot shot. She's a real fertile breeder, if you know what I mean."

Jack's temper roared in his ears. For just a moment he was blinded by it, Carmody's sly face dissolving in a red haze. Only the recognition of his anger kept him from driving that mop handle down Carmody's throat. Instead, he threw it down, letting the force of that action communicate the depth of his rage.

"Gol!" Cody exclaimed, his eyes nearly popping out of his head when he saw the tip of the mop handle shatter, one chunk flying across the room.

His hands free, Jack took a step forward, right into Heller. She levered herself against his chest. "Jack! Jack, don't! It won't solve anything, and it's what he wants. Please, Jack!"

As quickly as it had come, the anger retreated, at least enough to let a bit of reason slip in. He was about to break Carmody Moore into little pieces with his bare hands, right in front of his own children in their very home with their mother begging him not to. He took a step back, breathing deeply.

"Sorry," he muttered.

"No, it's not your fault," Heller said quickly, "but I think you ought to leave now. Okay, Jack? Will you do that for me?"

He nodded, thinking that he shouldn't have come in the first place. "You'll be all right?"

She smiled up at him. "Yeah, I'll be fine, promise."

He nodded again and shifted toward the door. Heller turned and literally shoved Carmody out of the way. Jack brushed by him and flung open the door.

"Mr. Tyler!"

Jack paused long enough to turn a look over one shoulder. Cody was on his knees at the end of the couch, his small hands grasping the curved back.

"Thanks, Mr. Tyler," he said huskily.

Jack nodded tersely and went out the door, wondering what Cody could find to thank him for. Maybe he was just grateful his father wasn't bleeding all over the place.

Jack pounded down the steps and headed for the street, fishing in his pocket for his keys. He could hear Carmody and Heller yelling at each other inside the trailer. Davy started screaming from the back bedroom, and Punk was getting in her two cents worth. *Oh, yeah,* Jack thought bitterly. He'd fixed things real well this time, him and his compulsions. He got in the car and drove away, trying not to think about what he'd left Heller to deal with all on her own.

Aw, Heller, what the hell am I doing? he thought. *Your daughter hates me. Your baby is scared to death of me. Your ex is causing you trouble because of me.* Seemed like Cody was the only one who had any use for him at all. But it was Heller who counted. He admitted it for the first time. He wanted her to want him—because he wanted her.

Heller sat down at the kitchen table and stared morosely at the dirty breakfast dishes. Boy-oh-boy, they'd really done it now. Punk was in the bedroom, pouting, banished finally for her rudeness. Carmody had made no protest about the punishment once Jack was gone, a fact that Heller hoped her daughter had noted. He'd been much too busy insulting Jack himself, as if he had any right to make judgments or pronouncements on any of her friends. Except she feared that she could no longer count Jack Tyler in that category, if ever she could have. No, whatever his reasons for showing up this morning, she doubted he would make that mistake again. They'd run him off for good.

To her dismay, tears filled her eyes, but she sniffed them up and swallowed them down, refusing to let even one fall. Her head pounded, and her stomach churned with disappointment, but she would not give in to it. After all, it wasn't as if she'd lost anything in Jack Tyler. She couldn't lose what she'd never had. Still...

She ran a fingertip around the rim of his coffee cup. He was such a thoughtful man, making her coffee, pushing aspirin down her, massaging her scalp and nape with his big, hot hands. She thought of how he'd separated Cody and Punk, of the authority in his tone and manner, the way he'd stopped Davy from eating dust from under her couch and then cleaned up after him. She chuckled, remembering the look on his face when Davy had let go. He liked kids, but he obviously didn't have much experience with the little ones. Pity he'd never had any of his own. At least she didn't think he had. No, he couldn't have. Any kid of his would be the center of his universe. She'd have heard all about him or her by now.

Heller sighed and got up from the table. She gathered up dishes and carried them to the sink, then started the water running. She sluiced out the sink, put in the stopper and squeezed out the soap. She stood for a moment watching the suds build and thinking. Why had Carmody had to show up right then? Why couldn't he have kept his smart mouth shut? She'd put the fear of God into him about just opening the door to her house and walking in without so much as a "Mother, may I?" The next time he tried that, she'd told him, she would go to court for a restraining order, even if it meant selling her car to finance such a venture. He'd seemed suitably cowed. It had occurred to her even then that Jack had done the very same thing, and it hadn't bothered her at all. It had, in fact, felt natural somehow, as if he'd belonged. Now that was a laugh, a man like Jack Tyler belonging in a shabby, crowded place like this.

She turned off the water and reached for a sponge. Unbidden and without warning, memory shivered over her. She closed her eyes and swayed against the cabinet. She saw herself sitting across Jack's lap, her head on his shoulder, his mouth covering hers, his hand at her breast. She felt the thrust of his tongue, the strength of his big body, the heat of that hand cupping her breast. Jack Tyler had awakened a craving in her she'd almost forgotten during nearly three years of chosen celibacy. She forced the thought out of mind, straightened and fixed her attention on the sinkful of dirty dishes.

"Mom?"

The small voice startled her. She looked down to find Cody standing close by her side. The expression on his face told her that he'd come to the same conclusion as she had about Jack Tyler. She steeled herself and began scrubbing a drinking glass.

"What is it, son?"

"Why'd Dad do that?" he asked. "What's he got against Mr. Tyler?"

She could have answered that in many ways, but she simply shook her head. "I don't know, Cody. I don't understand your father any better than you do."

Cody leaned a shoulder against the counter. "I bet Mr. Tyler wouldn't go around with other women," he said softly.

Heller dropped the sponge into the water, wiped suds off her hands and went down to eye level with her son. "Cody, I never meant for you to know about that. It's not right for a kid to have to know that about his father."

Cody screwed up his face. "I'm no baby, Mom. I even heard 'em sometimes, Dad and those women."

"Oh, God." Heller wrapped her arms around him and held him close. "I'm so sorry, honey."

"Wasn't your fault," he mumbled, and then he pushed away, looking at her with eyes more knowledgeable than any child's should be. "Mr. Tyler's not like that. I know he's not!"

Heller sighed and pushed up to her full height. "I'm sure he's not, Cody. I'm equally sure that Jackson Tyler has no real interest in me romantically." Not anymore, anyway, she added mentally. "You've got to get that out of your head, Cody. Otherwise you're going to be very disappointed." She plunged into the soapy water again, putting on her cockiest expression and trying to sound smug and bright. "Besides, I don't think I really want a man in my life right now, Cody. I like being independent, and we're doing okay, you and me. Together we're keeping this family afloat, aren't we? What do we need some bossy man for really?" She smiled down at him and winked. "You're man enough around this house for me, mister."

He smiled and puffed out his chest, but she could see the wistfulness lurking at the backs of his eyes. She felt it, shared it, but all it was good for was getting them hurt. She concentrated her energy on washing dishes.

"Go tell your sister she can come out now," she ordered dismissively.

He turned and moved lethargically toward the back of the house. Heller swallowed and scrubbed. She wouldn't cry. She absolutely would not cry, because if she ever got started, she might never stop.

Chapter Five

It was pure accident, but Jack was never one to question good fortune. He paused inside the door of the small café only long enough to signal Liz for a cup of coffee, which he carried over to the table where Carmody Moore was holding court. Jack knew the two girls at Carmody's table, and girls they were, one of them only fourteen years old. Both were part of the local cowboy culture and were always seen wearing boots, skin-tight jeans, and Western shirts with cutesy cutouts. Today was no exception. Both were hanging on every word that slithered out of Carmody's mouth. Jack stood at Carmody's back, sipped his coffee and listened.

"Yeah, now that night at the VFW," Carmody was saying, "that night was kind of an off night, you know? I mean, the creative juices, they just weren't flowing, and *that*, ladies, *that* is when making music is work. Everybody thinks music is just glamour and high living, you know, and yeah, some of the time, that's what it is, but I'm here to tell you, it ain't easy. No, sir, not just anybody can make a living at what I do."

Jack couldn't keep silent any longer. "That include you, Carmody? Is that why you're six months behind on your child support? Why your *three* little kids do without and live in a rundown old trailer? Why you don't even own a car?"

Carmody turned in his chair. "Tyler!"

Jack ignored him, smiling at the girls. "Hello, Amanda, Christine. Enjoying your summer vacation?"

Both girls visibly shrank. There was nothing like meeting a former principal to remind you how old—or young—you were. They murmured subdued greetings, sucked at the straws in their soda glasses and took their leave. Jack watched Carmody fume, relishing the moment, and seated himself at Carmody's table.

"How old are you, Carmody?"

"None of your business, big man," Carmody hissed. "Just 'cause you're hitting on my old lady, that doesn't give you the right to stick your nose into my business."

Jack set down his cup of coffee and leaned his elbows on the table, staring straight into Carmody's eyes. "Your *ex-wife* and I are friends, period. Now if you want to keep me out of your business, I suggest you stay out of mine, and that includes my relationship with Heller. And while we're at it, let me say this. If you ever insult her in my hearing again like you did the other night with your nasty innuendo, I'm going to take great pleasure in reshaping your face with my hands. The only reason I didn't do it then was because your children were there, and I have too much respect and concern for them to beat their daddy into a bloody pulp while they watch. But the message, in case you didn't get it, is this. You lay off Heller, or you answer to me."

"I'm not scared of you, big man," Carmody sneered.

Jack grinned. "No? Well, you ought to be, because I can't think of anything I'd rather do than put my fist through your face."

Fear flashed in Carmody's eyes, but he quickly covered it, adopting a well-rehearsed bravado. "You don't want to mess with me, Tyler," he said menacingly. "I know some of the worst bar toughs in Texas. You catch my drift?"

Jack chuckled, shaking his head, and no one would ever know how much it cost him to keep his tone steady and easy. "Yeah, I know a scare tactic when I hear one," he said. "Now I'm going to tell you again. You have nothing to say about who Heller sees or what she does. In fact, you better be sweetness and light with Heller from now on. Because if you hurt her, I won't be sending some fictitious tough guy after you, I'm going to be coming myself. And it won't be pleasant, Carmody, I promise."

Carmody squirmed in agitation, clearly frustrated by his inability to cow Jack with his smart mouth. "You think I've got no reason to question my ex?" he practically shouted. "Well, what about my children? How do I know my kids ain't suffering because of you? To hear Punk tell it, you're meaner than Simon Legree!"

Jack sat back and folded his hands in his lap, saying reasonably, "Punk's a six-year-old. All six-year-olds think principals are mean, but the truth is that school boards don't put people who dislike or hurt kids in positions of authority. Beyond that, I'd put my reputation up against anyone's. Fact is, I'm a nice guy—unless you cross me." He got up and thumped the table with his knuckles. "You'd best remember that." He walked away, keeping a tight rein on his temper, which for a moment there had threatened to get away from him. As compensation, he let Carmody pay for his coffee.

* * *

Fanny hacked and coughed and gasped and finally cleared her throat.

Heller noted the creases about her eyes and the pallor beneath too-bright rouge and felt a jolt of concern. "You smoke too much, Mama," she said softly, wiping down the countertop.

"Now don't start on me, Heller," Fanny complained in her gravelly voice. "I've got sinus. That's all it is. Besides, I didn't come down here to talk about me."

Heller sent her a blunt, knowing look, then turned away to wait on an old man buying a roll of toilet paper. He came in once a week and bought a single roll of toilet paper, never another blessed thing. He had the correct change counted out before the cash register finished chugging. Heller took it with a smile and wished him a good day. He said the same thing he always said, "Uh-yeah," and shuffled away. The door opened and a particular fellow came in. Heller hastily turned back to her mother, hoping he would just go away and knowing he wouldn't. No matter how many times she turned him down, he kept asking her out, and she'd have sooner dated Hitler. They were about even morally, but at least Hitler didn't have a beer belly that made him look as if the baby was overdue, and hair that surely hadn't been washed since Prohibition. Naturally he was a favorite of Fanny's.

"Hey, Boomer!"

He waved and headed toward the beer case.

"Don't encourage him, Mom," Heller said quietly.

Fanny leaned her elbows on the counter, displaying entirely too much liver-spotted cleavage in the process. Even this early in the day, her breath betrayed the gin she favored and increasingly denied using. "What have you got against Boomer? Your daddy always liked that boy."

"Dad would," Heller muttered. "They are definitely two of a kind, and he's hardly a *boy* anymore."

Fanny snaked a long, bare arm across the counter, charm bracelets jangling, to lightly prod Heller's shoulder with red-tipped fingers. "Maybe you got something else going?" she suggested, penciled brows arching.

Heller frowned. "What on earth are you talking about?"

"Don't play coy with me," Fanny said slyly. "I've heard all about it."

"Heard about what?"

"You and that schoolteacher."

Jack. Heller's heart slammed against her chest, but she knew better than to show Fanny such a reaction. She snorted. "Yeah, right. Can you see me with some nerdy little professor type?"

Fanny leaned a hip against the counter and folded her arms. "I hear he's some gimp—"

"Mo-ther!"

"Oh, all right, let's be politically correct then. I hear he's a *handicapped* fellow."

"He is not!" Heller retorted hotly, realizing her mistake too late.

Fanny smacked the counter with her open palm. "Ah-ha! Carmody was right! You've taken up with Cody's teacher."

Heller closed her eyes and tamped down her temper. "I haven't taken up with anybody, but if you're referring to Mr. Tyler, he's the elementary school principal, and he's definitely not handicapped. He has an old football injury that acts up sometimes, and that's all. There, now you know everything there is to know."

Fanny narrowed eyes shadowed heavily with neon blue. "I hear he's spent the night at your place."

Heller's temper went from simmering to laser cold. "That's a lie," she said, her tone deadly.

Fanny bristled, pursing a mouth gone crepey around the edges. "Don't you talk to me like that, my girl. I'm trying to help. I'm worried about you, Heller. A man like that Tyler can't want but one thing from you, and we both know what it is."

Heller laughed, but not because she was amused. "Why, Mother, I'm shocked. Aren't you the one who's always said that life without fun and games makes Heller a dull girl? And now you're worried because I might be playing some? Why don't you just say what you mean?"

Fanny puffed out her chest and folded her arms beneath it. "A man like that isn't for you, Heller. He can't have no real feelings for you. He feels sorry for you because you live on the wrong side of the tracks and you haven't got an education, but I know you, Heller. You think 'cause he pities you and he wants you between the sheets he's in love with you. Maybe he even tells you that, but you can't trust it, Heller. He's going to break your heart, girl, unless you wise up."

Heller shook her head, marveling that her mother didn't realize that she was breaking her heart now, as she had so many times before. Tears gathered in her eyes, but she'd be seventy and blind before she'd let them fall. "It's nice to know just how well you think of me, Mother," she said lightly. "I'm to understand that I'm not good enough for a man like Jackson Tyler, whatever he might tell me. Isn't that about right?"

"All I'm saying, Heller, is that if you count on him for more than fun and games, you're going to get disappointed."

Heller leaned forward. "Well, you don't have to worry, Mother, because there's nothing to this. Carmody's talking out of both sides of his head, as usual, and that's all it is, talk!"

"Carmody's not the only one talking," Fanny said complacently. "And where there's smoke, my girl, there's fire, you can count on it."

"Not this time!" Heller insisted. "You think what you want about me, but Jack Tyler is a kind, caring, decent man."

"Yeah, well, those kind gotta have it, too," said a new voice.

Heller turned on Boomer with fire in her eye. "I'm telling you he's not like that!"

Boomer raked bloodshot eyes over her suggestively. "He's a man, ain't he?"

"A gentleman!" she snapped, bracing both arms against the countertop.

"All that means," Boomer jeered, showing a broken tooth, "is he won't respect you in the morning, no matter what he tells you the night before."

Heller trembled with outrage. It was so unfair! They were talking about Jack as if he were a cold, scheming lecher! They seemed to think God had given *them* the right to make assumptions about that kind, good man: her mother, who had never denied herself anything she ever wanted, whether it be in bottles or jeans; and a man so shallow and degenerate that he actually believed he had a responsibility to moralize, for his friends, the sexual performance of any female stupid and tasteless enough to oblige him!

"You don't know what you're talking about!" she lectured, dividing her glare between them before settling it on her mother. "For starters, Jack and I aren't involved *that* way. Secondly..." She shifted her glare to Boomer. "A gentleman's thoughts and feelings are as foreign to you as Latin!"

"A gentleman is he?" Boomer sneered. "What kind of gentleman scopes out the mothers of little kiddies for a good time?" He slid a look at Fanny. "Wonder how many other skirts he's got under that way?"

Heller lost it. She had to go up on tiptoe and lunge forward to get a good swing, but she slapped him hard enough to actually send him staggering backward into the candy display. He dropped the bottled six-pack, spewing beer all over. "Get out!" she screamed. "Get out now!"

"God, you're crazy!" he exclaimed, but he said it picking his way hopscotch-style toward the door.

Fanny was bawling about getting her spandex pants and best red high heels wet, but Heller wasn't hearing any of it. "You, too!" She swung a finger toward the door imperiously. "And don't come back talking that filth!"

Fanny huffed and whined and struck belligerent poses, but she was retreating the whole while. "I was trying to help!" she proclaimed from the door.

"Lies don't help anyone, Mama!" Heller retorted.

Fanny stuck her nose in the air, whipped her bleached platinum hair off her shoulders and spun away. Agitation enhanced her wiggle to the point that she nearly fell off her stilettos.

Heller doubled up both fists and pounded the countertop. Damn that Carmody! He'd done this, and he'd done it for pure spite. Anger quickly gave way to despair as she thought over all her mother and Boomer had said. Dear God, Carmody was going around telling everyone that she was sleeping with Jack Tyler, and like her own mother, they were bound to think he was taking advantage of her. She closed her eyes, moaning at the full implication of what was being said.

Lake City was like every other little town in the world. Gossip was a main pastime. They'd tear Jack up one side and down the other, and a man in his position couldn't afford that! Heavens, what was she going to do? This was all her fault. If she hadn't accepted that ride from him, hadn't mentioned that she'd have liked to check on the kids, hadn't let him kiss her, he wouldn't have come back, Carmody wouldn't have walked in on them, none of this would be happening!

She wondered if Jack had heard the talk yet. If not, it was just a matter of time. She put her hands to her head, desperate to find a solution—for his sake. But what could she do? What could she do?

Jack was feeling pretty chipper. He'd stayed away five whole days, and this after putting the fear of God in Carmody Moore. His knee was feeling fine, which meant that he could walk almost normally, and for the last twenty-four hours he'd hardly thought about her, not more than five or six times, anyway, and never once on the golf course. Of course he'd only played nine holes. The guys had teased him, implying that he was saving himself for something—or someone—more interesting, but the truth was, golf just wasn't as much fun lately as it used to be.

Jack parked between two pickup trucks at the curb in front of the store and got out. As usual there were half a dozen people in the store. Most of them were kids, though, and like most kids, they grouped together, whispering and giggling and pretty much having fun. They recognized Jack the moment he walked through the door and filled the place with greeting.

"Hello, Mr. Tyler!"

"Hi, Mr. Tyler!"

"How are you, Mr. Tyler?"

He lifted a hand in greeting. "Well, hello, kids. How are you enjoying your summer?"

"Great!"

"Great!"

"We're playing volleyball down at the lake."

"Oh, that's fine. Have a good time. School will start again before you know it."

They made gagging, moaning sounds, which made him chuckle as he strolled around the counter to the side of the enclosure, which Heller had blocked off. He noted that she had thus far ignored him, but he put it down to her being busy punching out lottery tickets. He leaned against the counter and waited. Before long she finished with the customer. He caught her eye, winked and smiled.

"Can I do something for you?" she asked blandly.

He nodded, grinning. "I can wait, though."

She said nothing as she turned back to the other side of the counter. The kids all made complicated purchases. The boys went for tins of bubble gum meant to resemble chewing tobacco and little tablets of temporary, press-on tattoos, all of which had to be investigated to be sure that they were "way cool." The girls were more concerned with spending every penny in their possession without bothering to calculate anything, so that every time Heller gave them a total and they found that they still had money, they produced another piece of candy or bag of chips.

In the end Jack gave them seventeen cents to finalize the last purchase and get them out of there. The two men waiting to buy packaged sandwiches and cans of beans for lunch were grateful, so Jack magnanimously waited for them to conclude their business before claiming Heller's attention for himself again. He hoped to have a private moment with her, but the frequency with which customers kept walking through the door made that impossible, so he settled for what he could get.

"So what was it you wanted?" she asked almost disinterestedly.

He took that for an attempt to sound businesslike and leaned forward, keeping his voice low. "What I want," he said confidentially, "is to take you out. What do you say to dinner and a movie?"

Her expression for a moment was almost sad, but then that cocky, strong-willed Heller took over and she tossed back the long ponytail that had fallen over one shoulder. "Just when did you expect me to work in something like that, Tyler? Do they show movies at three a.m.?"

He had thought of that. "Don't you get a night off? It doesn't make any difference to me which night, you know. My time's my own for several more weeks now."

"Well, lucky for you," she said wryly. "My time, any free time that I have, belongs to my children. I'm afraid that dinner, the movie and anything or *anyone* else that takes me away from them is out. So—no, thank you." She turned away from him, smiled at a thin, middle-aged woman who wanted a pack of cigarettes and began chatting as if she hadn't just shot him down in flames.

Jack was too stunned for a moment to do anything but stare at her back. Then slowly the truth sunk in. She didn't want anything more to do with him. Probably, now that he thought about it, she never had, but he'd been too caught up in his own attraction to her to realize that. He turned away from the counter without a word and left the store. He was sitting in his car, blindly trying to fit the key into the ignition, when the full import of what had just happened hit him.

What a dolt he was! The woman had never been interested in him. He had shoved his way into her life without the slightest invitation from her, and he'd kept shoving his way in until, the very first time he'd given her an option, she'd calmly rejected him. It was Lillian all over again.

He'd been so sure that they'd been right for each other, Lillian the perky, blond cheerleader, him the varsity football player. She had been seeing the captain of the team, a guy whom Jack had known to be a bona fide jerk, so he had bided his time. Sure enough the jerk had dumped her, and Jack had stepped in to pick up the pieces. He hadn't waited for an invitation, and he hadn't taken no for an answer. He'd seen that she needed someone, and he'd decided to be that someone, period. Even after he'd dried her tears and sworn that she was the most attractive collegiate cheerleader in the nation, she had resisted him. But he'd worn her down. Right after he'd been named one of the top players in the nation and guaranteed a place in the professional draft, they'd gotten married, and for a little while, everything had been fine.

Then he'd blown the knee and the possibility of a pro career with it. Oddly enough, she had been much more disappointed than he had. He'd felt that it wasn't the end of the world. Football wasn't everything, after all, and he had his education to fall back on. But Lillian had never bargained for marriage to a schoolteacher. She'd vehemently denounced him for a failure and claimed that she could've had her old boyfriend back if she'd only tried, which, thanks to Jack, she hadn't done. It didn't help that the old boyfriend was quarterbacking an expansion team. Even then Jack had been unwilling to give up, though.

He'd honestly believed that his marriage had been worth fighting for, and he'd set out to win her all over again, even going so far as to take a job with her father's real estate firm. But they'd both been miserable. He'd hated selling real estate, and Lillian had hated being married to a disappointment. In the end he'd told her that he couldn't go on doing something he hated. He'd decided to teach, and he very much wanted to begin this new phase of his life with her at his side. If she couldn't be happy with that, however, he would give her a divorce and divide the assets they had acquired between them. She'd grabbed the money and walked away without the slightest compunction. She'd even taken a savage satisfaction in telling him that she had never loved him. She'd wanted to be married to a sport star, one of the American elite, and he had looked like a winner so she'd married him. But that was all he'd ever meant to her, and if he had just listened to her in the beginning, he'd have known that.

Well, at least part of that painful lesson had pounded its way into his head. He might have blundered into Heller Moore's life without thinking, but he wasn't about to follow up that colossal mistake with another. He could thank Lillian for saving him from making a total fool of himself for a second time. It was good to know that he hadn't suffered that experience for nothing. That knowledge did not, however, quite mitigate the very real pain he was feeling at the moment.

"Think of it as reinforcement," he counseled himself aloud. He'd think twice, thrice and more before pulling this stunt again. He'd finally learned the full lesson. He couldn't save the world, after all, and just because he was needed didn't mean that he was *wanted*. Most importantly, he must never ever again assume that just because he found himself interested in a certain female the feeling was mutual. In fact, he probably ought to swear off that kind of involvement for good. He apparently just did not inspire romantic thoughts in the opposite sex.

He started the car, backed it out and drove away, telling himself that this bleak mood would soon lift. He hadn't lost anything he'd ever really had, after all, and he had the satisfaction of knowing that he'd done some good, at least. If he hadn't actually lightened Heller's load permanently, well, that wasn't his problem. And only a fool would wish that it was.

She saw that she had hurt him. It was in his eyes. The pupils were so wide that they left only narrow bands of his green-gray irises, and it seemed to her that through them she could see straight into his heart. He was confused, and he was hurt, and in some indefinable way, he was embarrassed. She was trembling when she turned away from him, but she'd had lots of practice at maintaining that tough shell she'd encased herself in as protection against so much of the world. It was usually automatic, but not this time. She'd had to use a great deal of concentrated effort to keep to her course. And she was surprised at how very much she wanted to take it all back. If he'd spoken in those last awful moments, she feared she might have dissolved in tears of recrimination and apology. With relief and regret, she felt him walk away, and strangely, as soon as he moved away, she could not take her eyes off him.

She watched him grapple with her cold rebuff in a kind of horrified fascination. He just sat in the car for several long minutes, staring off into space, and as awful as she found the sight, she couldn't quite look away. It had mattered to him, *she* had mattered to him. Even after that awful scene with Carmody, he had still wanted to see her. She marveled at him and wished that it was not so. It would have been so much easier if he had washed his hands of her and kept his distance. To know that he was able to care so generously made him all the more attractive.

When at last he drove away, she silently pronounced herself free of guilt and regret. It was for his own good, after all. How else could she combat Carmody's vicious slander except to cut the connection? There was no point in continuing it, anyway. Nothing real or lasting could ever come of it, no matter how big a heart the man had, because as much as Heller hated to admit it, her mother was right.

Heller knew that she wasn't good enough for a man like Jackson Tyler. How ever she looked at it, she couldn't get away from the facts: she was a high school dropout of unsuitable background; she had three young children to support due to a very messy divorce; and she was still not free of the aftereffects of it. Her mother contributed to Heller's unsuitability. Indeed, Heller's parents were notorious in Lake City.

The family tendency toward alcoholism and wildness was well known. When her younger brother had died drunk behind the wheel of a fast car, before he was even old enough to acquire a driver's license, the consensus of the local community was that it was a miracle it hadn't happened even sooner. It seemed that the only ones shocked by what had happened were her parents. Heller still remembered with painful vividness how her parents had shown up at his funeral so plastered that the minister had angrily taken it upon himself to delay the service long enough to pour hot coffee down them until they could be trusted to behave properly.

That particular episode had been the talk around town for months. The buzz had finally begun to die down about a year later, but had been revived when, on the anniversary of her brother's death, her father had revived the gossip by literally drinking himself into a coma. He had died the next day. The official cause of death was listed as alcohol poisoning. Fanny seemed bent on following her husband down that very same path.

No, Jack didn't need or deserve her kind of trouble. He was a well-respected educator in the community, and she could not in good conscience allow herself to jeopardize that. She owed him too much to let that happen.

She couldn't help feeling a little sorry for herself, though. He had really been interested in her. It wasn't just the white knight in him, and she refused to believe that it was mere lust. He had actually asked her out on a real date, dinner and a movie. No man had ever taken her to dinner and a movie in the same night. Probably, no man ever would.

She went through the motions of taking care of customers, plying them with meaningless chatter and false good cheer, while telling herself that she had done the right thing. She could even be proud of having put his welfare above her own, especially as it would have been so easy to let him sweep her along in the wake of his generosity. If that didn't do much to ease the pain she felt, well, she supposed that time would eventually take care of it.

Precious time.

The one commodity of which she never seemed to have enough. No day was long enough, no week sufficient for its needs, while relief from the relentless effort of enduring always seemed months, *years* away. She watched her children's lives flying by, mired in regret because she seemed to share so little of it with them. She both longed for and dreaded the far-off day when their needs would consume less of her hard-earned salary and she could grant them more of her attention. Time was ever her enemy.

How ironic that it should now reveal itself as her only friend.

Chapter Six

She had known from the beginning that this day was not going to go as it should. First, Davy had been even more clinging than usual that morning. Not even Cody could coax the baby away from her. The little tyrant had literally sat on her feet with his limbs wrapped around her legs while she stood at the sink doing up the breakfast dishes. She could see no reason for it, and that worried her. Maybe he was getting sick. She'd watched him closely for any sign of his constantly recurring ear infection, but he hadn't pulled at his little ears or held his head to one side or seemed sensitive to noise, and he didn't have a temperature. She had devoted almost her entire morning to him.

Then, just to be certain that she didn't get any of the remaining household chores done, her boss had called and asked her to come in to the store ninety minutes early. Unfortunately she hadn't known that Betty had left the house without a word to anyone until *after* Heller told Mr. McCarty that he could count on her. She had reluctantly called her mother to fill in until Betty returned, only to hear Carmody's voice at the other end of the line. Her mother had spent the night with a friend, according to Carmody, after generously offering *him* housing for a few days. "After all," he had said importantly, "I am her favorite ex-son-in-law." In her chagrin at discovering fresh evidence of her mother's stupidity, Heller hadn't even bothered to point out to Carmody that he was Fanny's *only* ex-son-in-law.

That small grace had not kept Carmody from crying on her shoulder, however. It seemed that his roommates had kicked him out for failing to pay his share of the rent one too many times. Which, of course, was all Heller's fault for having "bilked" him out of half of his pay for that gig in Houston, about which she had had to remind him several times before collecting. He'd conveniently forgotten that he had used her car for transportation, not to mention the back child support that he still owed her. Heller hadn't mentioned those small facts, either, which may have induced the fit of human kindness that had resulted in Carmody volunteering to come over and watch the kids until Betty returned. Just to be on the safe side, however, Heller had slipped out of the house at the same moment Carmody had entered it, giving him no chance to beg for the money back. Now it looked as if they were both going to be out the money.

Heller looked at the steam boiling up out of the coils of her radiator and sighed. Why couldn't she get a break, just one decent break? She'd intended to use that money for outfitting the kids for school in the fall. Looked like Punk would have to wear her brother's hand-me-downs one more year, but that couldn't go on indefinitely. She firmed her jaw. No use borrowing trouble. Today had plenty. Tomorrow would bring its own. The immediate problem was to get to work. She would have somebody come after the car and repair it later. She left the hood up and went back to extract her purse and uniform from the front seat. Finding a ride to her second job was another problem she'd have to face later.

The temperature had pushed up into triple digits already, and she hadn't gone ten steps before perspiration had beaded on her forehead and begun trickling down the valley of her spine and between her breasts. She reached up as she trudged on and literally tied her ponytail into a loose knot to get it up off the back of her neck. It fell down moments later and she found that she had neither the strength nor the inclination to tie it up again. Four blocks later, she'd have gladly shaved her head, had that been an immediate option. Her blouse was damp and sticking to her, and her jeans were beginning to rub raw spots on her slick, sweaty skin. Maybe someone would offer her a ride before she was baked to a crisp.

As if in answer to that silent hope, a car swung around the corner just ahead and moved down the street toward her. She recognized Jack's sedan with heart-stopping delight. Was that man destined to forever come to her rescue? She felt a stab of guilt for the way she'd treated him that day in the store, even if it had been for his own good. Not for the first time she wondered if she should have simply told him straight out what was going on, but deep down she knew that he'd have refused her request to back off. No, she had done the right thing. She told herself that again as he drove right on by her without so much as a glance.

The smile that had fixed itself to her face slowly faded. She didn't realize for several seconds that she had come to a stop and had turned in order to follow him with her eyes. Abruptly she turned around and strode onward. Well, what had she expected? But she knew suddenly that she hadn't really expected it to end. Somehow she had believed he would still be there in some way. Bleakly she realized the full extent of what she'd done, and it had little to do with having to walk to work in the heat of summer. For a moment she mentally cursed Carmody Moore for being the catalyst for her disappointment, but then her roiling emotions began to subside, and she could admit that she had contributed handily to the mess her life had become. She swiped away the tears that mingled with perspiration on her cheeks and lifted her chin. She had survived worse disappointments, after all.

She had almost reached the intersection by the time Boomer pulled up next to her in his rumbling old truck. He leaned across the cab and pushed open the passenger door.

"Lucky for you," he said, all but sneering, "I ain't the type to hold a grudge."

Heller thought of slamming the door shut in his face, but it was another half mile to work, and she could see no good reason to walk it in the heat when a ride was at hand. She tossed her things inside, then climbed up after them, slamming the door shut. "Well, I am," she retorted, "so don't get any funny ideas."

She thought for a moment that Boomer would argue, but instead he sent her a dubious look and ground gears until he got the old truck moving. Heller sighed and propped an elbow in the open window. Could this day get any worse?

Jack held the image of a hot, bedraggled Heller in his mind for several moments before finding the resolve to push it away. He'd be a fool to play knight-errant again, knowing how she felt about him, not that seeing her again would make any difference to him at this point, but a man had his pride, didn't he? Why allow himself to be used? Besides, it was not as if she was in any real distress. She had surely lived in Texas long enough to become accustomed to its murderous summers. What business of his was it if she decided to take a stroll in the middle of the day? Some demon hidden deep within the recesses of his troubled mind cackled at that and pointed out what he had stubbornly refused to admit. She wasn't out for a little jaunt, with that familiar pale green uniform wadded up in her arms.

He had to tighten his hands on the steering wheel to keep from reaching out with needless guilt to shut off the air conditioner blowing cold into his face. What was this perversion that made him want to suffer just because she did? God knew she felt no compulsion to do the same for him. He passed her dinosaur of a car on the side of the road, its hood raised so that wafts of steam escaped into the already overheated air. He shook his head and stroked his mustache. That woman had the worst luck in the world. Car trouble was the last thing she needed. But that, he reminded himself sternly, was not his problem. Never mind that he'd have stopped if it had been any other female. Heller Moore was off-limits to him. She had as much as said it herself. He was going to use his head for once and keep his distance, no matter what his silly conscience said.

He switched on the radio, hoping to distract himself, and heard an announcer reminding the general populace that it was necessary to keep animals confined in shady areas with plenty of water handy in order to help pets and livestock avoid heatstroke. Pets and livestock, natural creatures that spent their entire existences out in the weather, this heat was dangerous even for them. And he had let Heller walk on, her delicate face flushed and clammy, her long, thick hair wet with perspiration.

When a ramshackle old truck passed him, he pulled to the side of the street and bowed his head against the steering wheel, yielding to the inevitable. After a moment he lifted his head, filled the chilled interior of his car with a long, audible sigh and started the car moving again. It would be easier to circle the block and pick her up than to turn around on this narrow street. He'd think about the problem with her car later.

He made two quick left turns and came to a stop at the very corner from which he had first spotted her. The old truck had stopped, and its driver had leaned over to open the passenger door and speak to her. With hardly a pause she tossed her belongings onto the seat and got in. A chill began at the top of Jack's head and shivered its way down to his feet. So much for the absurd notion that she needed him for anything. He should have known that the very next man to see her would stop—and that she would get in with him, perfect stranger or not, without the slightest qualm. Didn't the little idiot know that she could get in trouble that way? Well, it was nothing to him.

Gritting his teeth, he watched as the old truck shuddered and slowly pulled away from the curb. Heller stuck an elbow out the window and lifted the long tail of her hair off the back of her neck with the other hand. Having reached second gear, the truck promptly slacked off again and coasted to a stop at the intersection. Heller turned her head, and Jack felt the immediate impact of her gaze. Her eyes widened in recognition. Jack made himself relax back into his seat, one hand draped negligently over the steering wheel, his expression as composed and unconcerned as possible.

The driver of the truck, an overweight, balding fellow from the look of him, signaled Jack to come through the intersection by thrusting his hand out and bending his fingers in one rough, jerky wave. Jack leaned negligently in his seat and ignored him. Aware that his expression was no longer impassive, if ever it had been, he fixed Heller with a hard, uncompromising stare. The truck driver made a very unmannerly gesture, jammed the truck into gear and stomped the accelerator, causing the ramshackle vehicle to shudder nearly to pieces before it cleared the intersection and finally achieved second gear again. Jack didn't bother to wonder if it had a third as he watched Heller's face recede and disappear. She knew, of course, that he had been coming back for her. Chalk up one more stellar performance for the world's chief fool.

When the truck was well down the road, he swung around the corner and went on his way. Only after he'd pulled into his assigned parking space in front of his apartment did he remember that he had been going to the newspaper office to place an advertisement for volunteers to help with the fall reading program. He'd have laughed if he hadn't felt so miserable. What was wrong with him, anyway?

He'd decided to help her despite his better judgment, and he should be thankful that Heller herself had saved him from compounding his mistake. Truly he did not want to see or speak to her unless he had to, and clearly that was the path fate meant him to take. Why then did he feel as if he had been kicked in the middle by a particularly mean mule?

He pictured that rough character behind the wheel of the truck and Heller sitting next to him with her elbow poked nonchalantly out the window. A sinking sensation began in his chest and seemed to expand as it forced its way downward, congealing into a cold, heavy mass in the pit of his stomach. She shouldn't have been with that man. Why was it all right for her to be with that slime ball and not with him?

He jerked as if stung. No, he couldn't possibly be jealous of a guy like that. Firstly, he had long ago established the life he wanted, and no rough, ragged bum in a beat-up old rattletrap of a truck could possibly have anything he coveted. Secondly...

Secondly, he'd learned long ago that it was painful to be where he wasn't wanted, and the truth was that Heller didn't want or need him in her life. Her reason didn't really matter. All that was left for him to do was to accept the fact that he wouldn't be seeing her. And while he was at it, he might as well admit that he'd be envious of anyone who could claim her time, anyone at all—for a while. But only for a while. He made it a promise to himself. He would forget Heller Moore, no matter how long it took.

Heller absently fluffed her hair with her hands. She had soaked in the tub that morning. After the week she'd had, some pampering had seemed in order. So she'd filled the tub with hot, soapy water and just soaked—until Davy had climbed up to sit on its edge and splatter her with bubbles as he smacked his fat baby feet on the soapy surface. Knowing her interlude was over, she had steadied him with one hand and shaved her legs with the other, nicking the backs of both ankles while her hair tumbled down from its loose chignon and soaked up about a gallon of water. Punk had obligingly come in and coaxed Davy out of the room so Heller could wash her hair beneath the spigot.

Now she sat cross-legged on her bed, dressed in shorts and a matching sleeveless blouse with oversize buttons up the middle, a towel draped about her shoulders while she waited for her hair to dry. Davy clumped around the tiny room trying to keep her sandals on his feet.

It was her day off, but she wasn't thinking about the hundred and one things she could be doing around the house or with the kids. She was thinking about the look on Jack Tyler's face when she'd ridden by in Boomer's old truck.

Had he been coming back for her? She had been certain at the time that he had, but now all she could really focus on, all she could really think of, all she kept seeing over and over again, was the look on Jack's face. He had been hurt. He had assumed that she was with Boomer because she wanted to be, and that had hurt him because she had led him to believe that she did not want to be with him. She had hurt him twice now with that lie. Why hadn't she just explained? He was a reasonable man. He would have understood. He still might.

That notion had been flitting around in the back of her mind all morning, but she pushed it away, getting down off the bed to save her shoes from Davy by putting them on her own feet. She took his hand and together they walked down the hall past the bathroom and the other bedroom to the living area. Cody and Punk were lying on their stomachs in the middle of the oval rug, their chins balanced on the heels of their hands as they pored over the old storybook that Heller had picked up at a garage sale. Cody was reading aloud the captions beneath the illustrations, while Punk was busily spinning her own stories to go with them.

"The girl spun straw into gold," Cody read.

"I bet," said Punk, "that if she could spin straw into gold she could spin it into anything."

"So what?" Cody said, completely missing the point.

"So she'd spin up a bunch more than gold junk. She'd spin up TVs and wedding dresses and amusement parks and—"

"Naw, she'd just buy that stuff with the gold," Cody argued. But Punk was warming to her idea.

"No, listen, she could spin up a rocket ship and all the stuff she'd need to make a whole world, and she'd just blast off into space and leave that mean old troll behind. Then he'd try to get at her with magic, see, 'cept she'd have spinned up a magic wand of her own and a whole army of fierce girl warriors with their own magic wands, and when the bad guy came after her—''

''She'd zap him into a pile of gold dust!'' Cody cried, getting into the game.

Punk shook her head. ''No! She'd turn him into a pretty little girl that ever'body would love.''

Cody screwed up his face, liking his own idea better. ''That's dumb!''

''It is not!''

''Is, too!''

''That's enough,'' Heller said lightly, stepping over them to sit down on the edge of the couch. She bent and picked up the book.

''Read to us, Mom,'' Cody pleaded.

''All right.'' Heller smiled and thumbed through the pages, looking for something that intrigued her. Davy scrambled over his brother and sister, stepping on the bend of Punk's leg and the small of Cody's back before falling to one knee. He immediately began to howl. Heller laid aside the book and lifted him onto her lap, crooning, ''Poor knee, poor knee.'' She turned him upside down to kiss the hurt away, and his tears turned to giggles. Heller hugged him and picked up the book. ''Once upon a time,'' she began, pointing out the words with her finger so Davy could feel as if he was following along.

Her voice wove a tale of good that won out over evil, of magic and wishes and deeds fraught with peril. Cody and Punk soaked up every word, eventually coming up onto the couch to look at the pictures they already knew so well but never tired of seeing. Davy lay back against her, squirmed around a bit and finally drifted into a sound slumber. When the story was finished, she carried him to the room he shared with his brother and sister and laid him in his crib. Very carefully she worked a pair of elasticized plastic pants up over his feet and legs to his waist. A faint red smudge on one little knee reminded her of that minor accident—and Jack.

Was his knee paining him? Did he take proper care of himself, or did he just grit his teeth and bear the pain with a manly grimace? Did he have anyone to help him out when he was stuck in a chair with that leg propped up? Surely a man who did so much for others had friends and family lined up and just waiting for a chance to return a favor. But would he let them know that he was in need? She suspected not. In the same moment, hearing the front door open and Betty's muffled voice, Heller realized that her baby-sitter had come home earlier than expected after her night out. Now she had every reason to turn the tables on Jack Tyler. She knew where he lived; he'd told her the night he'd driven her to the nursing home.

She slipped out of the room and down the hall to snatch her purse and sunshades from the top of her dresser, then caught a glimpse of herself in the mirror and paused to pin up the sides of her hair. She hurried back down the hall to the living area. Betty was stowing a six-pack of colas in the refrigerator. She looked as if she'd slept in her clothes, and when she turned, Heller saw that she'd slept in her makeup, too. Her mascara was smeared, and the pale blue eye shadow she favored had been reduced to mere smudges in odd places. Heller frowned.

"You feeling okay?"

Betty shrugged. "Yeah, sure. I'm fine. We just had a late night, and I dropped off to sleep on Doug an-and Kitty's couch."

"Was the party fun?"

Betty smiled almost secretly. "Oh, yeah. *Great* party."

Heller had seen that sparkle in her eye before. "You met someone!"

Betty laughed. "Sort of." Before Heller could ask any more questions, though, Betty changed the subject. "You going somewhere?" She pointedly took in the purse, shades and pinned-up hair.

"Yeah, I thought I would, just for a few minutes."

"That's cool," Betty said, shrugging again. "I'll hang out here with the kids."

"You don't mind?" Heller asked anxiously.

"Nah, I got nothing else to do."

Heller relaxed and started for the door. "Davy's down for his nap. We've already had lunch. Leftover macaroni and cheese in the fridge if you want it." She paused at the door to speak to Cody and Punk, who were down on the floor with the storybook again. "Play quietly while Davy's napping, kids, and we'll take a run to the park after he wakes up. Okay?" They shot her pleased smiles. "I've got to go out for a bit, but I won't be long." They threw her hurried kisses, and she threw them back. Their noses were already buried in the pages of the book again. She slipped out of the door, satisfied that she wouldn't be missed for a few minutes.

Her old car, having had her few extra bucks poured into it, started up on the first try and took her without incident out onto the street and across town to the new apartment complex where Jack Tyler lived. She parked out of the way in a spot near the pool. A careful look at the adults, mostly women, sunning themselves at poolside told her that Jack was not among them. She checked the boisterous crowd of kids splashing in the water and tossing balls across the pool just to be sure Jack was not there, either, then hurried down the sidewalk to the two-story building that housed Jack's apartment, identified by the numbers posted on its side. His was the corner apartment on the first floor. With his knee, he wouldn't want to walk up and down those stairs every day. Thoughts of his bad knee gave her fresh courage. She walked up to his door and employed the brass knocker.

For a long moment she worried that he was not home, but a quick survey of the parking lot just beyond the terrace where she stood showed her his sedan parked nearby. She closed her eyes, sucked a deep breath, and lifted the knocker again. Before she could bang it against the brass plate, the door swung open. Jack stood before her wearing nothing more than a pair of gray knit shorts. His hair was wet and rumpled from a recent toweling, the towel still in his hand. Droplets of water clung to his eyebrows and mustache. He couldn't have been more shocked.

"Heller!"

Her heart thumped just once, very hard, and then seemed to drop into her stomach. Her courage plummeted with it. She stared, literally unable to take her gaze off the broad, molded plain of his chest. Oddly, he didn't look quite so huge without his shirt, and yet he positively oozed sheer physical power. Muscle bunched beneath his sleek, bronzed skin, smooth except for a narrow line of brown hair that began just below his breastbone and disappeared beneath the elasticized waistband of his shorts. Heller gulped and stepped back. "I—I caught you at a bad time."

"No!" He shot out a hand and captured her by the wrist. He released her just as suddenly the next instant, jerking his hand back as if burned. "Uh, I—I mean ... I was just rinsing off the, um, chlorine from the pool."

She nodded. "Oh." So he had been out there—with all those women. She felt her mouth turning down in a frown.

He stood like a statue for a moment, then looked her up and down as if he might discover by that means why she'd come to his door. She looked away and put a trembling hand to her hair in a bid for nonchalance. Abruptly he scrubbed the towel over his face and head and backed away from the door. "Come . . . come in."

Feeling like an utter fool, Heller glanced briefly at the parking lot, then put her head down and stepped resolutely through his door. He closed it and stood at her back. She nervously looked around her, anything to avoid looking at him again. She was standing in a small, tiled foyer, a coat closet right in front of her, the living room to her right, the kitchen to her left.

Recessed lighting in the kitchen showed her a dining area next to a bow window. The table was gray slate on blue chrome with four matching chairs cushioned with knubby gray tweed flecked with blue. Just beyond, a basket of fruit and a cookie jar shaped like a fat rooster lent a homey air to an otherwise pristine gray-and-white kitchen, but it was the refrigerator that captured her attention. She wandered in that direction, taking in the awkwardly colored drawings and the construction paper cutouts that were taped to every available square inch of the double door. Cody's advertisement was stuck over another coloring with a small magnet.

"You kept it," she murmured, walking across the small, gleaming room to smooth down the edges of the paper with her fingertips. "Along with all these others. My, you have quite a collection." She tilted her head, deciphering the printing on what was evidently a rendering of the school. "To Mr. Tyler, Best Prince-a-pal Ever. Gayle G." She smiled. "Clever."

"Gayle's a very clever little girl," he said, raking his fingers through his hair.

She shot him a quick look. "You really like kids, don't you?"

"It's why I do what I do."

"Yet you don't have any of your own," she heard herself saying and immediately regretted it.

"No one to have them with," he said succinctly.

She nodded, willing away the color in her cheeks.

He cleared his throat and said, "But you didn't come here to comment on my lack of family or to admire my art collection."

"No." She bowed her head, avoiding eye contact.

"So why did you come?" he asked softly.

She turned her head just far enough to take in his bare feet. Seemingly of its own will, her gaze climbed as far as his calves and then on to his knees. The left one was scarred and slightly misshapen, flat on one side, bulging gently on the other. She tossed her hair back off her shoulders, met his gaze and said, "I was worried about you."

He lifted a brow skeptically at that. "Oh?"

She swallowed, nodding. "I haven't heard from you in a while. I was afraid your knee was troubling you."

He slung the towel over one shoulder and folded his arms. Muscles bulged. Suddenly his chest looked a yard wide, his upper arms as big around as tree trunks. "No more than usual," he said. "In fact, it's probably better than usual. Swimming takes the pressure off the joint, lets me strengthen the musculature with less stress to the bone."

"Ah. I, um, didn't know that."

"No reason why you should. Now, tell me why you really came."

She opened her mouth, but closed it again when no glib excuse tumbled out of it. He shook his head in obvious disgust, turned, and walked out of the room. She followed him, feeling lower than a mole and just as lost. He walked into the small, cool living room and dropped down onto the far end of the fawn-colored sofa.

Heller took in the room with a glance, noting subliminally the butter-soft leather of the couch and matching chair, the unmarred glass tops of cubicle tables, the elegance of tall ceramic lamps with beige shades. Half a dozen trophies were displayed on the painted mantel of the small marble-fronted fireplace. Portraits of what could only be Jack's parents and siblings hung on the beige walls in silver frames. The wall opposite the couch was given over to an entertainment center complete with television, stereo, CD player, VCR and the latest video game console.

"Cody would have a heyday with a setup like that," she said too brightly.

Jack leaned forward, braced his elbows on his thighs and clasped his hands together, looking up at her. "Something up with Cody?"

She bit her lip, stepped over and took a seat on the end of the couch opposite him, tucking her purse into her lap. "He, um, keeps asking when you're coming over again."

His jaw firmed. He sat up and laid an arm along the back of the couch. "And did you explain that you had effectively told me to buzz off?" he said bitterly.

Heller crumpled inside. Her eyes filled and her nose plugged up with tears. "Jack, I'm sorry about that."

His voice sharpened. "Do you have any idea how I felt? You didn't just shoot me down, Heller. You chopped me off at the knees, *publicly.*"

"I know." The words were a whispered anguish. "At the time I thought it was the only way to deal with the gossip."

"What gossip?"

She looked at him in genuine surprise. "I thought surely you'd heard by now." She bit her lip pensively. "Maybe I caught it in time, after all."

Jack sat forward again, twisting to face her. "What are you talking about?"

She spread her hands over her knees, steadying both. "My mother came to see me. Carmody was going around telling everyone that we, you and I, were lovers."

He just stared at her, said nothing, did nothing, just stared blankly, and in that moment she knew that he didn't care a fig what Carmody Moore or anyone else said about him.

She felt a spurt of defensive anger. "I couldn't let them drag your name through the mud!"

He leaned toward her, splaying one big hand on the seat of the couch between them. "Heller, I'm an adult," he told her flatly. "I'm allowed to conduct my private life in any manner I see fit, within reason, and Carmody Moore has nothing to say about it. He can spread any lie he wants, but those who know me know I'm an honorable man, and they aren't going to judge me without hearing the pertinent facts. You might consider showing me the same consideration and stop jumping to conclusions about what's best for me and what isn't until you at least talk to me about it!"

Heller gripped her knees hard enough to bleach the color from her fingertips. "You don't understand! The Swifts and the Moores aren't the kind of people you can afford to be associated with. You're a good man, and your reputation ought not to suffer just because you decided to look out for me and mine."

He threw up his hands, sliding to the edge of his seat. "What are you talking about? Me and my reputation can take anything Carmody Moore wants to dish out. And as for the Swifts and the Moores, you and your kids are the only ones I give a flip about."

"You don't know our reputations, then."

"Oh, don't I? I know your old man was wild as a March hare. I know he drank himself to death after your kid brother was killed in a car wreck. I know," he said, "that your home life was hell and that you probably thought you were escaping it when you married Carmody."

She laughed unhappily at that. "All that did was pluck me up out of one gutter and land me in another."

"But you didn't stay there," Jack pointed out. "You climbed up out of it all on your own, and I'd say that was a pretty fair accomplishment."

"What you don't understand, Jack," she said desperately, "is that no matter how hard I work, there are those who will always see my parents in me."

"That's absurd."

"Maybe so, but that's the way it is. Every time Fanny gets so drunk she passes out at the table in some club or, worse yet, performs one of her infamous stripteases, I get the leers and the innuendoes at the store the next day. And even after all these years, some of my father's old friends are still waiting for me to revert to type. They say things to me, Jack, that they'd never say to one of the women teaching at your school, because the way they see it, the gutter's in my blood."

"Why do you care what they think?"

"I don't, not for myself. But for my children, Jack, and for you... My kids can't help who their mother is any more than I could, but you..."

He opened his mouth to contest what she was suggesting, but she silenced him with two fingers laid across his lips.

"There's one more thing," she went on softly. "About yesterday, Jack... I don't care what the others think about me, but I don't want you to think I was with that guy yesterday because I wanted to be. I just needed a ride. If I'd had one brain cell working I'd have realized that you were going to come back for me, but—" She dropped her hand to her lap once more, targeting her gaze on it. "I figured there was a limit even to your goodwill and kindness. And that's why I got in the truck with him."

"You're entitled to accept a ride with anyone you want," he said gruffly.

"I know, but normally I wouldn't give that jerk the time of day. Normally I wouldn't have accepted a ride from him under any circumstances, but..."

He was looking at her like she had her head on crooked.

She sighed. Well, she'd said what she'd come to say, and there was comfort in having said it. If he didn't understand, there was nothing she could do about it. She lifted her chin even as she rose to her feet and shifted the strap of her purse higher onto her shoulder.

"I just wanted you to know," she said again.

He nodded almost absently.

She made herself smile. "Well, I have to get back. Um, t-take care of that knee." She could see that he wasn't listening to anything she had to say anymore, so she didn't say anything else. She just turned and walked to the door. What else was there to say, anyway? She'd said it all, and now it was time to go. Her children were waiting. Her *life,* such as it was, waited for her at home, and she was ready now to get on with it. She walked through the door and closed it behind her.

Chapter Seven

He caught up with her on the terrace. It had taken him a moment to realize that she had actually gone, his mind was whirling so with all she had said and the implications of it. He was still reeling. Did she even realize that she had just exhibited more concern for *him* than for herself? He had thought that she didn't care, when the truth was that she cared more than he'd thought possible. How could she leave now? There was so much to say! He clamped a hand down on her shoulder. She jumped and whirled around. He looked down into that clean, pretty face, noting that her eyelashes glinted golden in the sunshine. He was smiling, his mouth stretched so wide it hurt.

"Where are you going?"

She wrinkled her brow as if she didn't get it. "What?"

He laughed at her confusion. "Suddenly you don't understand English?"

His hand had drifted up to her shoulder again, but she

sidestepped and shrugged out from under it. "Don't be stupid!"

He knew then that they had more to discuss than he'd realized. He sobered. "All right. I won't if you won't. Now answer the question."

She frowned and shifted her weight. He could tell she was feeling caught off guard. "I'm going home."

"Not yet," he said, stepping closer. "Come back inside." His hand skimmed up her arm, seemingly of its own accord.

She shivered and pulled her arm close to her side. "Why?"

He was becoming impatient, the need to touch her so strong that it couldn't long be denied, not that he had any intention of doing so. He curled a finger beneath her chin and tilted her face up. "Because I want to kiss you."

"What?" She literally recoiled, one hand coming up as if to ward him off.

He sighed. Was she going deaf? "I said—"

"I know what you said. I just can't believe you're serious."

"Oh, I'm serious," he assured her, and to prove it he pulled her into his arms and brought his mouth down over hers. For a moment she stood stock-still against him, and then, amid catcalls and hoots from the pool area, she abruptly pushed him away.

"Are you nuts?"

"Me?" he said, laughing at her dismay. "I'm not the one who wouldn't go back inside."

Her mouth dropped open. Storm clouds began building in those big blue eyes. *That's my Heller,* he thought delightedly, but he knew he'd better get her inside before the explosion came. He grabbed her by the wrist and literally pulled her into the apartment. She dug her heels in before he got her into the living room. He let go, closed the door and backed her up against it, in case she tried to bolt, which wasn't really likely considering how angry she was just then. But it seemed wise, anyway.

"What are you trying to do," she shouted, "ruin everything you've worked for? Didn't you hear anything I said to you?"

"I heard everything you said . . . every word," he told her mildly, planting his hands against the door, one on either side of her head.

She wasn't mollified. "I can't believe that you did that! What were you thinking, kissing me in full view of half the residents of this complex?"

"I was thinking that you're delicious," he said, leaning close.

Those blue eyes flashed dangerously. "Will you be serious? Don't you see that you just heaped fuel on the fire?"

"I hope so," he said, grinning despite his best efforts.

"It was bad enough that I even came here!" she went on heatedly. "But I felt I had to try to make you understand—"

His patience exhausted, he cut off the flow of words with his mouth, bending to capture hers and hold it until he got the reaction he wanted. For a moment, as before, she froze, and then she stiffened, going up on her tiptoes and lifting her hands to his chest as if to evade him or push him away. But it was a halfhearted effort, and he countered it by putting everything he felt for her and everything he *hoped* to feel *with* her into that kiss. She rewarded him moments later with a moan of sheer helplessness as her body melted against his and her arms slid about his neck.

He felt like celebrating, like hopping around the room and pumping his arms and maybe spiking a ball or something, but that would mean letting go of her, and the compulsion to keep this woman in his arms went far beyond any other. Just holding her, in fact, was not enough. He didn't really know what would be enough for him as far as this woman was concerned, but he had every intention of finding out. With that in mind he scooped her up and carried her to the couch.

She had enough presence of mind to lift her head and gasp, "What are you doing?"

He dropped down onto the middle of the couch with her in his lap and buried his hands in her hair on either side of her face. One of the pins with which she'd secured it popped free and fell onto the cushions. "I'm trying to tell you something," he said, tilting her face, just so. He could see her pulse beating rapidly in the hollow of her throat.

"What?" It came out all breathy and soft.

He put a kiss between her eyebrows and pulled back to look deeply into those blue eyes, burning now with a different kind of fire. "I'm trying to tell you that I don't care what anybody says or thinks about us. All I really care about is *you.*"

The fire in those eyes changed to a warm glow. "Jack. Jack, that's so sweet, but I can't let you—"

He dropped his hands to her upper arms and shook her lightly, just once. "You've had your say. I listened. Now it's my turn." He let his smile soften the sternness of his voice, his hands skimming over her shoulders and up the smooth column of her neck to her face. "I know my own mind, Heller. I'm not stupid."

"I know. I shouldn't have said—"

He pressed a thumb against her mouth. Such a tempting mouth. "I'm not self-destructive. I'm not impulsive...not too impulsive, anyway. The point is, I know what I'm doing."

"And what is that, Jack?" she whispered, her lips brushing the pad of his thumb.

"Exploring," he said, no longer able to keep his gaze off her mouth. "It's been a long time since I felt anything like this, Heller, and no one's going to stop me from finding out just how deeply these feelings run—not even you, now that I know why you pushed me away."

He brought his face close to hers, his nose gently nudging, his warm breath billowing softly between them. Her eyelids fluttered shut. Her hands tightened on his shoulders. He tilted his head just so and pressed his mouth to hers, feeling the whiskers that framed his upper lip twitch. She made the most deliciously inarticulate sound containing both wonder and welcome. Any doubts he might have had evaporated, leaving only the compulsion, rich with need and desire, to touch and taste and discover. He wanted to know every erotic secret of her body, to test the very limits of pleasure with her. He wanted to make himself a part of her and her a part of him, so much so that there could be no question of belonging. He didn't really think that was possible just now, but he meant to take it just as far as she would let him.

The very thought of taking her with him where he wanted to go was enough to ignite wildfires burning in his veins. He deepened the kiss commensurately, plying her mouth with more expertise than he'd even known he possessed, and when she opened for him, he spiked his tongue into the creamy hollow she provided him. She made that sound again, and sensation exploded in him.

He felt acutely the way her thighs nestled against his hardness and the soft press of her breasts against his chest. She wound her arms around his neck. He dropped his hands to her chest, pulling back just enough to slide them down over her breasts to her ribs and lower still to encircle her waist. He was trembling when he slipped one arm around the small of her back to brace her and splayed his free hand over the gentle mound of her belly, pushing downward until his fingers slipped into the steamy crevice between her legs.

She gasped and arched her back over his arm, breaking the kiss. He slid his mouth over the curve of her jaw and down her throat, allowing his mustache to lightly brush her skin, while his fingers fumbled with three oversize buttons on the front of her short, fitted blouse. She shivered as the buttons released one by one, and he peeled the blouse back and off, his teeth nipping the blade of her collarbone. His hands found the catch in her bra and worked it free, then skimmed the straps off her shoulders and down her arms before laying her back against the cushions.

His own lungs were working like bellows as he feasted his eyes and filled his hands with the perfect mounds of her pale golden breasts. Her rose brown nipples peaked beneath the sweep of his fingers. He bent low and kissed a particularly appetizing cherry red mole on the inner slope of one breast, then trailed his tongue up that slope to capture the peak at its crest. She cried out, her fingers tangling in his damp hair. He took as much of her into his mouth as he could, forgetting that his mustache might abrade her delicate skin, forgetting everything except the need to join their bodies. He had to get her out of her clothes. He brought his hands down to the waistband of her shorts and began struggling with snaps and zippers. Impatient to the point of desperation, he straightened to look down at what his hands were doing. It was his first—and last—mistake.

He felt the change in her almost instantly, even before her hands began pushing his away.

"Oh, my God!" Her legs flailed as she struggled to sit up.

"Heller, wait!" He pressed her down again, prepared to plead, if necessary. But a look into her eyes told him to keep the words behind his teeth. The smoky haze had cleared from those twin skies, and storm clouds were once again gathering. He shifted his hold and pulled her up into a sitting position, her legs draped over his lap. She twisted out of his grasp and scrambled up, hitting him in tender places with various moving body parts. "Ugh. Oof!" He made a grab for her wrist even as he doubled over and missed.

She snatched up her blouse and danced back out of reach. "I can't believe this! What were we doing?"

He lifted a brow at that. "Making love?" He pushed his hair off his forehead and looked up to find her struggling with the hook on her bra. She was utterly glorious, lush, beautiful—and completely flustered.

"We can't do that!" she exclaimed, tossing her blouse over one shoulder so that she could concentrate on getting her bra hooked.

Jack got up stiffly and moved toward her. "Here let me do that."

She shot out a hand to ward him off. "Don't touch me! That's what got me into this!"

He grinned. "Yeah, I noticed. Now come here." She batted at his hands, but he ignored her, grasped her by the shoulders and turned her. He snagged the ends of her bra band and brought them together. She jumped when his fingers brushed her back as he made the connection. He stepped back. "All done. You can yell at me now."

She threw her blouse around her shoulders, stuck her arms through the sleeve holes and yanked it together before turning on him. "I'm not going to yell," she grumbled. "It was as much my fault as yours."

He brought his hands to his waist, trying valiantly not to smile. "No, no. I take full responsibility."

Her eyes narrowed dangerously. "But you're not the least bit repentant, are you?"

The grin broke free. "Not in the least."

"Oh!" She pushed her hair out of her face and glared at him. "You rat. And I thought you were such a nice guy."

"I am."

"Well, for your information, I'm not some easy conquest you can just drag into your bed at first opportunity, no matter how much I might want to be there!"

He knew that if he laughed she'd probably slug him, so he clapped a hand over his mouth, delighted to know that it was her principles that stood in the way and not her desires. "I—I'll remember that," he managed to say, but she was too wound up to pay him much heed.

"You think I'll do anything you want just because I like you more than anyone else... and because you look like some kind of Greek god standing there in your—" She gulped, looking adorably confused as her gaze raked over him. "W-well, I won't!" She snatched her gaze away and began thrusting those huge buttons through their holes. "Even if it means never getting to— That is, I won't sleep with you ever unless..."

"Unless what?" The word *married* leapt into his mind, and he shocked himself by almost saying it, by almost suggesting that they consider it. Fortunately she wasn't in any mood for conversation.

"The point is," she stated firmly, "it's not going to happen, not like this."

"All right," he said, lifting his hands in complete capitulation. "And now that that's out of the way, when can I take you out?"

Her eyes widened in surprise. "You...you want to see me again?"

"Again," he said. "As often as possible. Anytime we can manage. Just tell me when."

She stared. He could see the battle she was waging and knew that just *because* she battled he had already won this particular skirmish. Still, she shook her head. "I—it's not a good idea."

He sighed and pointed out the obvious. "Look, I can't make you go out with me, but I can promise you that you're going to get awfully tired of closing the door in my face if you don't."

"I—I can't."

He folded his arms and gave her his best authoritarian glare. "Not an acceptable answer."

She was crumbling right before his eyes. "No, really, I—"

"Don't have any choice," he finished for her, "because I'm not going to compromise on this. How's tomorrow night?"

She shook her head. "Working."

"When's your next night off?"

"Not till Wednesday."

"Fine. What time can I pick you up for dinner?"

"Jack, I can't. I have so little time with my kids."

"They can come along."

She laughed. "Yeah, right, I can just see us trying to have dinner with Davy crawling all over me and Cody and Punk arguing over every little thing."

"We don't have to go to dinner. We'll do something else."

"Like what?"

He shrugged. "We'll think of something. I don't really care what."

She bit her lip, then said, "I guess I could maybe make dinner for you. We wouldn't have to go anywhere, would we?"

He'd have crowed if he hadn't been afraid of putting her back up again. "Sounds great. Shall we say about six?"

She wrinkled up her nose. "Seven might be better."

"We can always split the difference," he suggested. "Six-thirty?"

She smiled. "Six-thirty will be fine."

Gotcha! he exulted silently, and this time he wasn't at all certain he was going to let go, no matter how hard she pushed. He'd been mad to think that she was the wrong woman for him. Now all he had to do was convince her. He no longer worried that he might be repeating the same mistake he'd made with Lillian. If that turned out to be so, well, he'd deal with it then. Better that than never to have tried; to have lost by default this special woman.

She heard him as he climbed the steps to the door and panicked. Blindly she continued shoving serving dishes full of food into the oven, turned off the heat, slammed the door and straightened, pasting a smile on her face. Jack knocked on the door, and she marveled that she could hear it over the pounding of her heart. Punk could hear it, too, but she sat at the end of the table, scowling, and ignored it. Heller willed her feet to move toward the door, but somehow she couldn't make them move. What if he scooped her into his arms and started kissing her right there? Her pulse rate quickened at the thought, but she was painfully aware of Punk sitting there. She wouldn't want her little girl to see her make a fool of herself over a man she shouldn't even be seeing. She thought of calling for Cody, who was keeping Davy occupied for her, but realized that Jack would hear.

"Get the door," she insisted in a whisper to Punk, who scowled a little harder. "Go on!"

Punk slid from her chair as Jack knocked again and dragged her feet a whole yard to the door. Moving at the same speed as a lazy, octogenarian snail, she grasped the doorknob, turned it and tugged open the door an inch at a time. Jack literally slipped sideways through the narrow opening she allowed him and jumped back out of the way as she slammed the door shut with surprising strength. Jack smiled at her obvious hostility.

"Well, hello, Miss Moore. Nice to see you again, too."

Punk put on a vicious face, lip curled up in a silent snarl. Jack chuckled, his mood buoyant.

"Where's your mom?"

Punk lifted an arm and pointed into the kitchen. Jack turned in that direction, smiling warmly. Heller kept her distance, lifting one hand in a little wave. His gaze moved over her appreciatively, returning to her face to fasten on her eyes and communicate intense private longing. Heller gulped, tingling in places about which she was embarrassed just to think. Suddenly Jack frowned, his brows drawing together.

"Something burning?"

Heller started, simultaneously surprised by the question and aware of a faint, smoky scent. She whirled toward the stove and cried out at the wisp of smoke leaking from the top of the oven door. The signal light told her that she had not turned the oven off but had turned it *up,* all the way to broil. She spun the dial—to the right position this time— with one hand and yanked open the oven door with the other. A puff of smoke and steam hit her in the face, but she still saw that the top of her meat loaf was black and her creamed peas curdled.

"Oh, no!" She grabbed for a hot pad with one hand and the sizzling casserole with the other.

"Heller, don't!"

Jack was there even before the pain in her left hand made her release the dish of peas. The small casserole hit the floor.

An arm wrapped around her waist, Jack yanked her back before the hot cream splattered her. Her feet dangling above the floor, he turned her to the sink, wrenched on the cold water and stuck her hand beneath it.

"My meat loaf!" she wailed.

"It's all right. I'll get it. You just keep your hand under the water." He released her gradually and backed away, only to bump into Punk. "Go in the other room, hon. I don't want you burned, too." Punk, miraculously, did as she was told. He found two pot holders, carefully squished his way through the peas and retrieved the remaining dishes from the oven, placing each carefully atop the stove.

Cody and Davy hurried into the room before he was through, brought by the sounds of catastrophe, and he shot a quick look at Punk. "Keep them out for me, honey. We've got quite a mess in here."

Punk promptly spread both arms and placed herself at the end of the table. Heller turned off the water, dried her hand and began pulling paper towels off the roll.

"What a mess! My dinner's ruined. The whole evening's ruined!"

Jack tossed away the hot pads and turned to pull her into his arms. "Nothing's ruined. Besides," he whispered, "this is what I came for. I can get food anywhere. Only here can I finagle a way to get you into my arms."

She chuckled, pleased to the tips of her toes, then shoved him away, all too aware that her children were watching. Sighing, she went down on her haunches and began wiping up peas with the paper towels in her hands. Jack wisely took the roll from the holder and squatted beside her to help.

"We can still go out for dinner if you want," he told her as they worked.

She bit her lip. "I'm not really hungry, anyway."

"What about the kids?"

She got up and poked at the meat loaf. Only the top was blackened. Everything else had been on the bottom rack and so was fine. "I think I can salvage enough to feed them—and you, if you're interested."

"That's fine," he replied lightly, swiping up the last of the peas while Heller reached for the mop.

She sent him into the living room while she mopped the floor. No sooner did he sit down on the couch than Cody and, surprisingly, Davy began crawling all over him. Punk retreated into her former silent hostility, glaring at them all. Heller cut the top off the meat loaf, covered it with ketchup, and transferred it to the table, which she then pulled away from the wall to make room for Jack. She carried the remainder of the meal to the table and called everyone in to eat.

Everything was fine until all were served and Jack began trying to make conversation. Cody responded enthusiastically, too enthusiastically, really, while Punk glared and Heller tried to smooth over her poor manners and see to it that Cody ate his dinner. Davy, unfortunately, began feeling left out and decided to include himself in the conversation by letting out an ear-splitting screech, which made the kids laugh, Jack cringe and Heller scold him. His next gambit was not so easily dismissed. He squashed meat loaf and ketchup into his hair, getting chuckles from everyone but Heller this time, who cleaned him up with a paper towel. Meanwhile Punk tried to hide her cooked carrots under the edge of her plate. Heller admonished her mildly and got murdered with a look for her restraint. Her patience wearing thin, Heller dished up a second serving and insisted that Punk eat it. To her dismay and Punk's disgust, Jack commiserated with Punk.

"I only eat them because they're good for me," he said, popping one into his mouth and making short work of it. "I actually prefer mine raw and crunchy."

Punk rolled her eyes and chewed sulkily. Heller closed her eyes and counted to ten. Davy launched a handful of carrots at Jack's chest and hit him on the cheek and chin. In the ensuing silence, he waggled his little brows, clearly anticipating the laughter that had been the result of his earlier antics. When it did not come, he smacked himself in the eye with mushed carrot and began to wail. Heller didn't know what to do first, peel the carrot off Jack's chin or shush Davy.

While she dithered and apologized repeatedly, Cody expressed outrage at Davy's behavior, accusing Punk of enlisting him in a campaign to make Jack hate them all. Punk took violent exception to that, shouting and kicking Cody beneath the table. Heller began scolding them all, while Jack reached up with his napkin and removed the carrot from his face. Calmly, at first, he began asking everyone to quiet down and intermittently grew louder himself while trying to assure Heller that everything was fine. Finally he brought both fists down on the table, rattling every dish, glass and piece of flatware, and shouted, "Stop!"

The room went dead silent. Davy peeked out between his fingers. Heller closed her mouth, embarrassed again, and both Cody and Punk slumped in their chairs. Jack cleared his throat, picked up his knife and fork and muttered, "Eat your dinner."

The muted clinks and clatters of civilized dining replaced the chaos. Heller cleaned Davy's hands and began feeding him herself. Could anything else go wrong? she wondered. It'd be a miracle if Jack ever came back after this—but then she'd said that before. And she was supposed to want him to stay away. Only she didn't. So naturally this time he probably would. That would make Punk deliriously happy, make Cody very sad, and break her heart. Blast! Was there no winning? Jack's voice brought her out of her reverie.

"Uh, Heller . . ."

She turned away from Davy, spoon suspended in midair. "What?"

He merely inclined his head in Davy's direction. Heller looked back to her youngest son. He was chewing energetically, his eyes switching back and forth between her and Jack, his cheeks puffed up like a little chipmunk's with the excess of food she'd blindly poked into his mouth. She dropped the spoon.

"Oh, for—" She grabbed up a napkin, intending to make him spit into it, but Jack caught her hand and gave an almost imperceptible shake of his head. Davy seemed to catch every nuance of the byplay, and while she watched, he grew from a big baby into a little boy, his little jaws working like jackhammers until finally, he gulped, sighed and grinned— at Jack. Jack grinned back, winked and reached across Heller to ruffle Davy's curly hair. Davy beamed, leaned across the tray of his high chair for the spoon that Heller had dropped on the table and began to eat with all the dexterity of a four-year-old. Jack chuckled and tucked into his own dinner. Every so often, he would glance at Davy, who'd smile and keep eating as if some silent communication known only to the two of them had been passed.

Cody watched the interaction between his brother and his principal with bald hope, while Punk first stared, then returned to her glare, but not, Heller noted, before something very like jealousy flashed over her face. Suddenly Heller understood that her beautiful, prickly little girl was as afraid of opening her heart to Jackson Tyler as Heller herself, as afraid and as desirous. She wanted to like him;

she just didn't want to be hurt again by a man who almost seemed too good to be true. Almost, but not quite.

Heller thought of what had happened between them the last time they'd been together: how he'd stripped her to the waist and reduced her to a puddle of jelly before she'd even realized what was happening; how he'd smiled at her as if utterly delighted when she'd announced that she would not sleep with him; the way he'd pressed her for this dinner date and disavowed any concern for the gossips or his reputation or anything but her. No, he wasn't perfect. He was flawed in exactly the right ways. Her heart sped up, and for the first time she felt real hope. But that was a dangerous emotion and one she meant to crush—as soon as she figured out how.

The remainder of the evening passed without incident, or at least without making any incident seem larger than it actually was. Jack insisted on helping her cleanup, so the two of them bumped around in the kitchen while the kids pretended to watch television instead of them.

Afterward, he decided to go. Cody and Davy came to say goodbye, Cody receiving a pat on the back that plastered him to Jack's side. Davy demanded to be picked up, jabbering as if Jack just naturally understood every unintelligible word, while his fingers explored Jack's mustache. Apparently satisfied, he kissed Jack on the nose and allowed himself to be put down. Jack bade Punk a polite farewell and contented himself with an answering grunt before turning to Heller. She'd been wondering if he was going to kiss her, but even when he slipped his arm about her shoulders and pulled her close she didn't know for sure. Only when his mouth briefly pressed to hers did she have her answer, and then he was thanking her and slipping through the door, promising to see her again soon.

She closed the door behind him and turned to her family with a smile. Davy ran around the room in circles, jabbering to himself, before finally bolting down the hall. Cody beamed her a delighted smile and went after his brother. Heller chuckled to herself. Maybe this could work after all. Stranger things had happened. Punk was quick to burst her bubble.

"Well, I think he's a pain," she announced smartly.

Heller tried not to snap. "You made that abundantly clear."

Punk seemed determined to push her, though. She leaned back on the sofa and fixed Heller with narrow, knowing eyes. "If you just gotta have a man to kiss you," she accused, "why don't you let Daddy come back home?"

Heller's temper flared. She heard herself saying, "Carmody's no man. He's a *boy,* and he always will be."

Punk looked, for an instant, as if she'd been slugged. Heller's stomach turned over. Contrition flooded her. She plopped down on the couch next to Punk.

"I'm sorry. I shouldn't have said that."

Sullen, Punk hunched a shoulder in dismissal. Heller picked her next words carefully.

"It isn't about kissing, Punk. It's about sharing and caring and, most of all, trust."

"Daddy trusts you!" she said, swiping tellingly at her face.

"Maybe," Heller said. "He trusts me to take care of you and the boys, I think. But there's a deeper kind of trust, Punk, where you trust someone not to hurt you, and neither Carmody nor I can do that with each other."

"Why?"

Heller sighed. "That's a private matter between your father and me."

"'Cause he went with those other women?" Punk asked astutely.

A chill shivered through Heller. "Yes. Because of those other women."

"Don't you think old Mr. Tyler would do that, too?"

Heller shook her head, determined suddenly that her daughter understand the importance of fidelity. "Not every man cheats on his wife, Punk. Don't you ever let yourself believe that. Every wife—and every husband, for that matter—has the right to expect loyalty. Without that there can be no trust, and without trust you can't have love, Punk."

"Do you love Mr. Tyler?" Punk asked, her chin wobbling.

Heller felt her heart drop again. "I—I don't know for sure, Punk. I think I might, if he... That is, I think Jack's still trying to find out how he feels about me and what that means to him."

"Are you gonna get married if he asks you?" Punk pressed, frowning.

Heller caught her breath. "I—I... N-no one's talking about marriage, Punk! Goodness, I'd just like to be able to get through an evening together without everybody screaming at each other."

Punk sighed and propped her head on her fist, her elbow digging into the sofa cushion. "I don't want to yell," she muttered. "It just happens."

Heller looked at her daughter with a kind of hopeless compassion. "I know, honey. I have that problem myself sometimes. But it's important to try."

Punk nodded without enthusiasm and slid off the couch to the floor. Falling on her stomach, she propped her chin up in front of the television and reached for the remote control, effectively dismissing both the subject and her mother. Heller let her, simply because she didn't know what else to do or say. Why, she wondered, her hope extinguished, couldn't anything ever be simple?

Chapter Eight

Jack's smile faded as he viewed the clerk behind the counter. He was absolutely certain that Heller was supposed to be working now. He felt a prickle of unease. Something was wrong. Heller didn't miss work unless something was wrong; she simply couldn't afford to. He took a long look at the short, wiry, cigar-chomping, fiftyish man in her place and decided that he seemed unlikely to give out information on demand. He seemed unlikely, in fact, to be polite.

After a moment's consideration, Jack decided that it would be best to ask any questions casually. To that end he took a can of iced tea from the walk-in cooler and got in line behind an old woman buying paper plates, and two little girls trying to come up with enough coins to pay for a loaf of bread and two pieces of candy.

The cigar man rubbed a stubby hand missing two fingers over his bristly white hair and grimaced around the soggy butt clamped between yellow teeth. "Have you got the money or haven't you?" he demanded of the girls. One of them sent a trembling, doe-eyed look at him and continued searching her pockets. Pleasant fellow, Jack thought wryly. Fishing a quarter from his pocket, he stepped forward and placed it on the counter. The little girl with the doe eyes looked up, flashed him a smile of recognition and giggled thanks. Jack was unsure of the child's identity, but she was definitely familiar. He winked and stepped back into place.

The man behind the counter scooped up the coins, counted out six cents change and slapped it down out of the child's reach, apparently intending it for Jack. The girls hurried out of the store, their purchases clutched in sweaty hands. Jack mused that the least the man could have done was give them a paper sack, but he kept that opinion to himself.

The elderly lady in front of him offered to let him go first, evidently in appreciation of his generosity to the girls, but he smiled and shook his head, then popped the top on the tea and slugged back half of it while she paid for the paper plates and the man with the cigar glared at him. To buy himself a few moments conversation, as well as to irritate the curmudgeon, Jack paid for his tea with a twenty-dollar bill. The guy shot him a glare, picked up the six cents and threw it back into the cash register before painstakingly counting out change for the twenty. Jack leaned a hip against the counter and guzzled tea.

"So where's Heller today?" he asked in what he hoped was an offhand manner.

The cigar shifted from one corner of a frown to another. "Don't never hire a woman with kids," he grumbled. "It's always something."

"And what was it this time?" Jack probed, fighting back a spurt of alarm with a chuckle.

"Damned baby-sitter run off, she says." He waved that three-fingered hand dismissively. "But if it wasn't that, it'd be something else."

Betty. Well, well. Jack sipped more tea. "I thought Heller was pretty dependable. A woman in her position can't usually afford to miss work."

"Yeah, well. She don't come to work tomorrow, I'm gonna have to replace her." The man plucked the cigar from between his teeth, grimaced and stuck it back. "I can't stand catering to these cruds around here."

So the bad-tempered man was Heller's boss. Good grief, was there any indignity or irritation that poor woman didn't have to endure? Jack finished the tea, crushed the can and tossed it into the trash bin on the other side of the counter, saying, "I'm sure she'll work something out."

"She better," the fellow grumbled as Jack scooped up his change, stuffed it into his pocket and left the place.

"Well, hello." Heller stepped back and allowed Jack entrance into her home, Davy perched heavily on her hip.

He smiled, ruffled Davy's hair and dropped a feather-light kiss on her cheek. "What's this I hear about Betty running away?"

Heller rolled her eyes. "That goose has taken a powder with her best friend's husband! Can you believe it?"

"You mean, she was the other woman?"

"Evidently."

"Holy cow."

"Meanwhile, I'm left high and dry."

Jack chuckled and spread his arms. "What does that make me then?" Davy apparently took his stance as an invitation and, holding out his own arms, lunged at Jack. "Whoa!" Surprised, Jack scooped him up and brought him against his chest.

Heller laughed and wrinkled her nose in astonishment at her son. "You fickle thing. All morning long you've been stuck to me like skin, then as soon as a better ride comes along, you abandon me!"

Jack loosened his hold on Davy somewhat and made an obvious effort to relax. Davy pulled a wet finger from his mouth and stroked Jack's mustache with the intense concentration of an entranced scholar. Heller shook her head. "Well, you've worked your magic on him," she told Jack wryly.

He grinned. "Good. Then we'll get along just fine while you're gone."

She cocked her head. "Gone?"

He shifted Davy to his side, holding him safely with one arm. "I went to the store before coming here."

"I assumed that."

"Pleasant fellow, your boss."

She smirked and folded her arms, striking a doubtful pose. "Yeah, right, and crocodiles make good house pets. What'd Mac say to you?"

Jack settled a compassionate look on her. "He said that if you didn't come in to work by tomorrow, he'd fire you and hire someone else."

She put both hands in her hair. "He must not have found anyone to fill in for me. Blast! He hates working the counter."

"I noticed."

"I have to find Mother!" She whirled away, grabbing the phone mounted on the wall above the counter that divided the kitchen area from the living area. Agitatedly she punched in a series of numbers and waited, her fingertips drumming on the countertop. Finally she slammed the receiver back into its cradle and gave an inarticulate cry of sheer frustration. "Where is that woman? She never leaves her house before two. She doesn't even get out of bed before noon!" She smacked the countertop with the butt of her fist.

"Hey." Jack carried Davy over to her, positioned himself just so, and slipped an arm around her shoulders. "She'll show up eventually."

"But I need her now!" Heller insisted.

His arm tightened. "It's okay, honey."

Her anger receded in a flood of warmth that came with the sound of concern in his voice. "You're right," she agreed, succumbing to the temptation to lay her head against the hollow of his shoulder. "McCarty will just have to wait. Surely I'll find her before tomorrow."

"Frankly," Jack said, "I don't see the need for either one. I'll stay with the kids. You go on to work."

She straightened and looked up into his face. "I can't do that."

"Why not? Might make McCarty think twice next time there's a crisis. At least he'll know you won't take advantage."

"But I would be," she said. "I'd be taking advantage of you."

"No way. Look, it's not like I have anything better to do."

"Yeah, right, as if baby-sitting someone else's kids was just what you had in mind for the day."

"Maybe not," he admitted, removing his arm from about her shoulders in order to tickle Davy's belly where it peeked out from beneath a too-small T-shirt. Davy clapped his hands over the spot and giggled. Jack smiled. "But it could be fun."

Heller shook her head and reached for Davy. "No, really, I can't let you do that." To her surprise, both Davy and Jack pulled back, Davy snuggling possessively against Jack's chest, one little arm curling around his neck. Heller's mouth fell open in surprise. Then she narrowed her eyes at her son. "Traitor."

Davy grinned around a trio of fingers and said, "Yack ickel muh."

Heller poked a finger playfully at his tummy and said, "Well, Mommy tickles you, too."

He grinned but pushed her hand away and laid his head against Jack's chest again. "Yack," he insisted firmly.

Jack chuckled, and at the sound rumbling up from deep in his chest Davy raised his eyebrows. "Well, I've got this one in my corner."

"Don't forget Cody," she muttered, remembering how her oldest son had actually suggested that perhaps she ought to call Jack, when they'd realized what Betty had done.

Jack patted Davy's back and said wistfully, "Now if I can just get your daughter to like me."

"Good luck," she told him ruefully.

Jack reached out to smooth the fall of her hair. "Maybe this time on our own will help."

She wrinkled her nose, thinking that he knew all too well how to get around her. He apparently took the expression for disapproval.

"On the other hand, if you don't trust me..."

"It's not that!"

"Maybe you'd just rather leave your mother with them."

She rolled her eyes. "Actually," she admitted, "I don't like to leave them with my mother at all. You're by far the more responsible sitter."

"Well, then?"

She looked at Davy snuggled against his chest, sighed and capitulated. "It'll only be until nine. I've managed to cover myself at the nursing home this evening."

He smiled and slowly bent toward her, bringing his face close to hers and saying, "Great. Then we'll have the evening to ourselves." He kissed her lingeringly on the mouth. Davy babbled something about "Yack ickeling Mommy" and then closed his pudgy little hand in Heller's hair, pulling until she tilted her head back.

"Ow! Jealous little monster." She lifted the hem of his T-shirt and kissed him noisily on the belly, while Jack gently pried his fingers free of her hair. "I've gotta get going," she said, once free. Then she turned to hurry toward her bedroom and plowed straight into Cody and Punk.

Cody was beaming, an excited, hopeful glint in his eye, while Punk maintained her usual scowl. Heller knew in an instant that they'd both witnessed that kiss, and to her surprise she felt her cheeks begin to burn. A quick glance in Jack's direction showed that he had carefully composed his own expression into one of unconcern. For once, she decided, she was going to let him handle the repercussions.

She dropped quick kisses on her son's light brown head and her daughter's light blond one, then announced, "I've got to go in to work, after all, kids. Jack's going to stay with you, but I'll be home early. You be on your best behavior."

Cody agreed brightly. Punk scowled. Heller beat a hasty retreat, changed her shorts for jeans and was out the door before she could think twice about leaving Jack to the mercies of her two obviously adoring sons and her glaringly hostile daughter. She reflected guiltily that she hoped Jack had sense enough to keep the knives out of reach. Otherwise he'd need stitches before she got back.

It was actually fun, even though Punk—what an awful name for a little girl!—did her best not to enjoy herself. After Davy fell asleep in his lap and was tucked into bed, Jack decided to entertain himself in the only way that seemed open to him, since the other kids were in determined possession of the television. He made a quick trip out to the car, pulled his putter and a can of balls from the golf bag in the trunk and went inside again to set up a little putting green in the hallway with a piece of carpet and a plastic cup. The first time the ball made that distinctive rattle in the cup, Cody came to see what was going on. A discussion of the fine art of putting followed, and Jack found himself letting Cody try.

The putter was much too long for the boy, of course, but Jack tried to teach him the basics, anyway. When he looked up sometime later, it was to find Punk watching with wistful concentration. Expecting her to turn up her nose, Jack offered her the putter. To his surprise she not only took it, she allowed him to correct her stance and grip and guide her through the swing. To his utter amazement she not only sunk the first putt but the second and the third, as well. In fact, it seemed that as long as she stood in that exact same spot, she could sink those putts indefinitely. Jack studied her solemnly then said, "I think I'd better take you golfing."

She studied him back, then finally nodded just once.

Jack called the store and informed a harried Heller of his plans. She thought he was insane but didn't actually forbid him to take the kids out, as long as he waited until Davy woke up from his nap. There was a lengthy delay when Davy woke to a wet bed, Jack having failed to put plastic pants on him. Davy had to be bathed and changed, then the bed had to be stripped and the bedding washed in the bathtub. By the time he got the sheets and pads rinsed and got up off the floor, his knee was killing him. He ignored it, beyond swallowing some of Heller's aspirin, and hustled the kids, a safety seat and a change of clothes for Davy into his car.

Cody and even Punk, though she struggled hard not to show it, were wildly appreciative of his car. It was the first "new one," according to Cody, in which they'd ever ridden. Jack didn't tell him that it was three years old, know ing that would point up the decrepitness of their mother's twenty-plus model.

Jack put the car on the highway and headed toward Dallas. On the outskirts of Lewisville, they passed a popular fast-food place with a very visible sign. Davy gasped and immediately began struggling with his belts, babbling something Jack could not discern. Cody interpreted.

"He wants a kiddie meal. They got toys in them."

Jack glanced at the dashboard and saw that it was nearing dinnertime. "You guys hungry?"

Even Punk admitted that she was. Jack exited the highway and doubled back.

Once inside the building, Jack mechanically ordered a super-deluxe burger and super fries for himself and three kiddie meals. Cody tugged on his elbow and answered his questioning glance with a solemn pronouncement.

"Punk and me don't usually get kiddie meals."

"Oh? How come?"

Cody glanced at the clerk and said uncomfortably, "They cost too much."

Jack looked at the menu board and in moments calculated that the kiddie meal, in special container with toy, cost a grand total of sixty cents more than the burger, fries and cola sans container and toy. That came to a buck twenty. Had money ever been so dear for him as it was for Heller and her kids? He looked purposefully at the clerk, a pimply teenage boy, and said, "Oh, well, it's too late now. It's already been punched into the computer. Right?"

The teenager winked. "Right."

Jack thought he heard a distinctly feminine gasp of delight, but when he looked down, Punk was staring disinterestedly out the window. Cody, however, curled his small hand gratefully around Jack's larger one.

It took some doing to get Davy fitted into a high chair and then to pry away two of the three kiddie meals, which he had hugged to himself with gleeful toddler greed. Jack then found himself struggling to get food down youngsters more interested in playing with new toys, however cheap, than eating. Davy especially delighted in putting his toy on his head and then waggling it until the toy fell on the floor. Then he would whine until Jack returned it to him, only to repeat the process.

By the time they were back in the car, Jack was having second thoughts about this outing. But it was impossible to disappoint these kids, especially when they were already acting as though they'd just finished a tour of Disneyland. Punk's scowl had even been temporarily displaced by a carefully blank expression that failed to obscure the gleam in her eyes.

That gleam intensified when, equipped with a putter just her size, Punk soundly beat Cody at a game of miniature golf. Jack gave up any thought of competing about the fifth time he chased down Davy and brought him back to the proper green. The sixth time, Jack threatened exasperatedly to tie the little stinker to him, at which point Cody informed him that Heller often did just that. Emboldened and desperate, Jack went to the attendant at the desk and inquired if he might have a length of soft, cotton cord. The attendant did him one better, producing an actual tether, complete with small, zippered harness. Jack was sheepishly relieved to know that he wasn't the only adult who had this problem.

No sooner was Davy zipped into the harness, which was then clipped around Jack's wrist, than the little tyrant decided he'd really rather ride on Jack's foot than run around. The game then became one of trying to get a putt past Davy without it being grabbed or kicked astray. By the time they left the miniature golf park, Jack figured he could play the movie version of Frankenstein without rehearsal, he'd dragged his kid-laden leg around so long. His knee was throbbing intensely, but he felt a warm, glowing delight in the day. He didn't have to wonder if the kids enjoyed themselves, either.

Even Punk, who hadn't expressed one word of gratitude to him personally, gushed to her mother about her prowess with a golf club and went so far as to fail to sneer at him when he elaborated on her obvious gift for the game. Cody was positively beaming, and Davy, who went eagerly into his mother's arms, babbled incessantly about "Yack" and proudly displayed his fast-food toy. All in all it had been a fine day, and as Jack watched Heller make herself an egg salad sandwich, he anticipated a fine evening. Heller was tired but smiling as she parked herself on the sofa next to him.

"You saved my life today."

"That's what friends are for."

She cut him a narrow, smiling look. "Friends, hmm?"

He slid an arm around her shoulders, grinning down at her. "Maybe a little more than just friends."

Punk got up off the floor at that and plopped down next to her mother. As if in support of Jack, Cody took a position next to him. Not to be outdone, Davy crawled up and sprawled across both Jack's and Heller's laps, babbling around the fingers that he constantly thrust into his mouth.

Heller shook her head, laughing, then slowly sobered. She laid her head back against his arm. "Well, we got through today," she said. "What about tomorrow, though? I can't let you sit my children every day, and I can't afford to lose my job."

"I have some ideas about that," he told her. "I know some trustworthy young women who could be counted on to watch over things around here."

"Oh, that's great. I was going to put an ad in the newspaper, but this is better. I won't have to worry about a babysitter who comes with your recommendation."

"Hey, I think I've just been complimented," he said, grinning.

Heller lifted her nose. "Don't be silly. That wasn't a compliment, just a statement of fact."

"Yeah? Well, just how hard would you have to work to make a compliment out of it?"

Heller sighed dramatically. "Ask me later, when I'm not so tired."

He laughed and stroked her arm lightly, more than merely complimented, when she laid her head in the hollow of his shoulder and settled in to stare at the television. Jack waited expectantly as one by one the children dropped off to sleep.

"I think it's bedtime," he whispered delightedly, more than an hour later. He lifted his arm from about Heller's shoulders and gently scooped up Davy's utterly limp body, but as he slid to the edge of the seat in preparation for rising and looked back over his shoulder at Heller, it was to find her sleeping as soundly as exhaustion demanded. So much for his delightful evening.

Jack chuckled to himself as he quietly put Davy to bed, remembering the plastic pants this time, then gently roused the other children and urged them into pajamas and bed. Cody was the soul of cooperation, settling happily into the upper bunk of a rather rickety set of beds that Jack was determined to strengthen at first opportunity. Punk was glum but either too tired to protest when he tucked her in or actually warming up to him. He was almost afraid to think that it might be the latter, but he had hopes.

With the children down for the night, that only left Heller. After consideration, Jack decided to let her stay where she was. She roused slightly when he eased her down onto the sofa, mumbling something about the kids and school. He smoothed back her hair and lightly kissed her cheek, whispering, "The kids are fine, honey. Get some sleep."

She sighed and folded her arms against her chest. He eased off her shoes, then found a lightweight blanket to spread over her. Going down on his haunches next to her, he ignored the pain in his knee and studied her face for a long while. Was this extraordinary woman his destiny? He hoped so, for he'd never known a more valiant, more determined, harder working female in his life, and something told him that if ever she allowed herself, she would love with all the ferocity of a lioness. He wanted to be loved like that. He wanted to make life better for her and her kids. More than anything else at the moment, however, he wanted to slip beneath that blanket with her and slowly awaken her body with his own. But he knew that the time was not right, so he contented himself with a kiss brushed across her tempting mouth.

She sighed and breathed out a single word. "Jack."

His heart stopped, then took up a slow, heavy, almost painful throb. He heard himself whispering, "I love you," and in that instant he knew that it was true. What would happen with them? Could she learn to trust again? Would she yield him her heart?

Questions without answers. And yet, he mused, if ever a man might find his destiny drawn and posted in crayon, it was Jackson Tyler. That thought in mind, he switched off the television and reluctantly left her, careful to lock the door behind him as he took himself off to a bed that somehow no longer felt like his own simply because she wasn't in it.

* * *

Heller smiled at Mary Beth Kern and offered her hand to seal the deal. Mary Beth smiled back, pretty despite the braces and freckles, and shook Heller's hand eagerly. "Thanks, Mrs. Moore. I'll do a good job, I promise."

"I'm sure you will," Heller answered.

Mary Beth whirled, golden hair flying and swooped down on the kids. "Want to go outside and show me around the place? I bet we can make a neat fort out back!"

"Yeah!" Cody and Punk scrambled up, stuffed their bare feet into shoes discarded only minutes earlier and rushed to the door. Meanwhile Mary Beth coaxed Davy into her arms and propped him on her hip. When the door opened, however, and it became apparent that Mary Beth meant to take him outside, Davy balked.

"Yack! Yack!" he called, opening and closing his hands, arms stretched out toward his new favorite, who sat at the end of the dinner table.

Mary Beth carried him over, and Jack took him into his lap. "He likes you, Mr. Tyler," Mary Beth observed.

"Yeah, we're old buddies." He tickled Davy's tummy where his perpetually too-small T-shirts left it exposed. Davy collapsed back into Jack's arms, giggling and flailing his arms and legs, his reaction entirely too jolly for the effort expended by Jack.

"Is it okay if he stays in here with you while the rest of us go out and play?" Mary Beth asked.

Jack patted Davy on the bottom. "Sure."

But Davy suddenly suffered an attack of toddler's capriciousness. Bawling, "On go! On go!" he flipped over and practically crawled up Jack's chest, launching himself at Mary Beth. Everyone laughed as the tall teenager caught him and swung him onto her hip.

Heller snatched his sandals from the counter and thrust them at Mary Beth. "Better put these on him."

"I'll do it before I let him down," she promised and herded her charges out the door.

Jack shook his head. "You'll like her. I'm glad she was available."

"So am I," Heller said, leaning against the end of the counter, "especially since she's willing to work for less than I was paying Betty." She said nothing of how she was going to manage the evenings, since Mary Beth would not be sleeping over. Heller figured that she could bully her mother and Carmody into helping out until she could work out something else, though what that was going to be, she couldn't imagine at present. She smiled to cover her concern and asked, "Want some tea? It's cold."

Jack shook his head, a slow heat in his eyes. He lifted an arm and hooked a finger in the empty belt loop of her jeans, tugging her forward to stand between his legs. Heller knew it was folly to tempt fate like this, but she couldn't help putting her hands upon his shoulders and smiling down at him. He reached up with his other hand and clamped it around her nape, pulling her down until her mouth met his. Sighing, she let her eyes drift closed and rubbed her lips against his.

Chuckling, Jack wrapped his arms around her and pulled her down onto his lap. He crossed his legs, trapping her between them, and lifted a hand to stroke her hair. "We need to talk," he said huskily.

Heller nodded, but as she slid her arms about his neck, her gaze fell to his mouth. "Later," she whispered.

Jack groaned as he answered her invitation, grinding his open mouth against hers and filling its soft, sweet cavern with the restless sweep of his tongue. She pressed herself against him, feeling his hardness from thigh to breast. Oh, he enticed her so easily to this fine, hot madness. If she didn't develop some resistance, she was going to find herself in a very untenable situation, the kind of situation that a woman of her experience and maturity could not justify.

Reluctantly she pushed away. He let her go just as reluctantly, his hands following to skim over a hip and up an arm. She backed up against the end of the counter and caught her breath. "I, um, have to change into work clothes."

He gave her a crooked grin. "Need any help?"

Laughter erupted. "If I did, I'd lie about it! You're much too much a temptation."

"Am I?" Pleased, he leaned the chair back on two legs, locked his hands behind his head and propped his crossed ankles on the corner of the table.

"Stars, I'm going to regret that," she muttered.

He gave her a wolfish grin and wink. She threw up her hands, then escaped down the hall, laughing at the way her heart pounded at the promise in that wink. Lord, he made her want what she couldn't have, and he didn't even have to touch her to do it. She shook her head in wonder. Once she had believed that this was how it was meant to be, how it would always be between a man and a woman, but then experience had convinced her otherwise. She saw clearly what she had not wanted to admit even to herself: it had never been like this with Carmody.

Carmody had been a haven from the chaos and uncertainty of her parents' home; not a safe haven, as it turned out. Eventually the situation became as chaotic and uncertain as the one she'd fled, but she had felt duty-bound to be the best wife she could be to him. How much easier that would have been if Carmody had lit this kind of fire in her. Suddenly she was asking herself if her tepid response to Carmody might have driven him to other women. If that were so, might she not trust Jack in this circumstance not to grow tired of her?

She pushed both thoughts away and pulled a newer, darker pair of jeans from her cramped closet. As she shimmied out of the old ones and into the newer ones, she asked herself if Jack would find her so attractive if he could see the stretch marks on her belly and breasts. They were pretty mild, really, just a shiny pink line here and there. Still, Jack could surely have his pick of women—one more thought on which she did not want to dwell. She switched her attention to more immediate problems.

Sitting down on the edge of her bed, she reached for the receiver of the old rotary dial phone on her bedside table and laboriously spun out her mother's number. Fortunately Fanny answered this time. Heller then spent several difficult minutes alternately pleading her case and biting her tongue as Fanny complained about the imposition and everything else that came to mind. Heller assured her mother that the imposition would be temporary and finally got off the phone by saying she was going to be late for work.

When she emerged from the bedroom, purse in hand, it was to find the kids piled up on the living room floor with Mary Beth, Davy standing at her back with both arms wrapped around her throat and jumping up and down with glee as she described a game they were to play. Jack looked on benignly, his elbows propped on his knees. He got up as Heller caught Mary Beth's eye and gave her a little wave to indicate that she was leaving. Together they slipped out the door and down the steps. There they should have parted ways, but he took her by the elbow and walked her to her car, where he kissed her quickly and said, "See you later, hon."

It never occurred to her that he meant that same night.

Chapter Nine

Jack hummed to himself as he climbed the stairs in the gathering dusk, limping slightly. He paused on the stoop, rapped once, then opened the door and went in. The living room was empty.

"Mary Beth? Kids?"

He heard a door open in the hallway. Shoes clacked on the linoleum, accompanied by a faint metallic jingling, and then the most astonishing woman appeared at the entrance to the living area. Jack felt his jaw beginning to drop and quickly clapped a hand over his mouth and pretended to clear his throat. The woman struck a kind of slouching pose, her hands—complete with purple press-on nails—were poised at the waist of a clingy purple dress, cinched in with a yellow belt at least five inches wide. That was about the length of the skirt, too. The dress also featured a plunging neckline and tight sleeves that ended just below the elbow. On her arms she wore heavy, gold bracelets, fitted with dozens of jingling charms. Her bleached blond hair was pinned on top of her head in piles of stiff, frizzy curls, exposing clumps of charms dangling from her ear lobes almost to her shoulders. She wore purple and yellow shadow on the loose lids of bloodshot eyes, which matched her bloodred lipstick all too well. And on her feet were purple shoes—which unfortunately were not a good match with the dress or the eye shadow—with ankle straps and stiletto heels at least six inches high. It was a miracle that she could stand up in them, let alone walk.

She cracked a mouthful of chewing gum, looked him up and down and said, "Who the hell are you?"

Jack dropped his hand, shocked to his toes and a little angry. He took a step forward. "Where are Mary Beth and the children?"

She gave him another of those insulting once-overs, then shook out long legs, still firm enough to belie the droop of face and breasts, and clacked her way across the floor. "Little Mary Beth has gone home to her supper," she said, picking up a pack of cigarettes from the counter. "Heller ain't here."

Jack cleared his throat and dropped his hand. "I know where Heller is. What I want to know is where the children are." As if in answer, he heard the pounding of smaller feet, and suddenly Cody was throwing himself at him.

"Jack!"

"Hey, bud!" Jack stooped and caught up Cody in his arms, standing with him in one smooth motion. "What's up, son?"

"We didn't know you were coming!"

"No? You should have. Did you think I'd leave you on your own all night?"

Cody directed a significant glance at the now-smoking woman, leaning negligently against the counter. "Granny Fanny is here," he said rather dispiritedly.

Fanny. So that's Heller's mother, Jack thought, watching the woman's heavily penciled brows rise and her red-rimmed eyes roll in obvious disapproval of being called anyone's granny. No wonder Heller married so young! he concluded.

"So you're Jackson Tyler," the newly identified Fanny mused. "Well, you're a lot of man, I'll give you that. Too much for Heller Suzanne." She rolled a hip out and parked a hand on it. "I knew you'd be outta her league. What do you want with my girl, anyway? As if I didn't know."

Jack felt his temper rise. He bent and set Cody on his feet. "Maybe you should go check on your brother and sister," he said firmly.

Cody shot a look at Fanny, then nodded. As he moved warily back in the direction from which he'd come, he said to Fanny, "You're not s'posed to smoke in here."

"I'm not supposed to smoke in front of you kids," Fanny retorted in her gravelly voice, "so get on out of here, and keep them other kids in the bedroom till I tell you to come out."

Jack gulped in an effort to keep sharp words from escaping his mouth. His hands curled into fists. "I don't appreciate your insinuations."

Fanny smirked. "Honey, I don't make insinuations." She sashayed across the room to the little bookcase stuck in the corner at the end of the couch, bent far enough to scare the dickens out of Jack, as her tiny skirt rose up the backs of her thighs, and plucked something off the top shelf. She carried it back across the room and offered it languidly at arm's length.

Feeling stupid somehow, Jack took the softly bound papers in hand and glanced at them, recognizing a SAT registration packet and sample test, the very materials available to every high school student in the state. His first thought was that Mary Beth had left them behind, but then he saw Heller's name scrawled across the bottom in ink. Heller was studying for the SAT? He felt a surge of pride. Of course. She was astute enough to realize that a college education might be her only hope of getting out of the rut in which she worked and lived. He smiled to himself.

"I knew it!" Fanny's voice accused. "You put her up to this nonsense, didn't you? Got her hopes up when God and all creation knows she ain't got a chance in hell!"

"I didn't know anything about it," Jack said offhandedly.

Fanny ignored him. "I've been expectin' something like this. I told that girl that you wouldn't do nothin' but complicate her life!"

Jack almost laughed. As if Heller's life could get any more complicated or difficult than it already was! He tossed the booklet onto the countertop and addressed Fanny Swift.

"I think you underestimate your daughter. She's smart enough to know what it takes to get ahead in this world, and God knows she's not afraid of hard work."

"And look what it's got her!" Fanny exclaimed, thrusting out her arms to the jangle of her bracelets, one hand holding a smoldering cigarette. She pulled it in and took a puff, blowing the smoke out in a brisk stream. "Three kids hanging on her skirt tail—if she had a skirt—and a run-down old trailer. Thing's a damned fire trap in the winter." She puffed again. "I'd take her in, you know. Kids, too." She smirked, a fair imitation of Mae West, and slyly added, "Carmody's already living with me."

"My sympathies," Jack muttered.

Fanny shrugged. "Carmody's all right. He likes his fun same as any man, you included."

"My idea of fun and Carmody's are different as night and day."

She looked down her nose at him, blowing smoke. "I bet."

Jack shrugged. "Think what you like."

She leaned one hip against the counter. "You're wasting your time," she said. "Heller ain't never had the least inclination toward fun. No wonder her life's so tough."

"Her life's so tough," Jack said flatly, "because she made a bad choice in desperation and because no one's ever done right by her."

Fanny straightened. "I resent that!"

"So do I. And I resent you standing here in her own house criticizing her when you ought to be proud as punch of the way she chooses to conduct her life! Heller works hard for her kids and herself. She takes pride in what she does, and she loves those kids more than anything else in the world. She wants to better herself for their sakes, and you call it nonsense. That's the very kind of thing she's had to overcome all along, and by golly, she's done it. She's nearly worked herself to the bone in the process, but she can damn well hold up her head in any company! She deserves support for that, and I, for one, intend to see that she has it."

Fanny was looking at him like he'd grown a second head. "You don't say?"

She clearly didn't have the least notion of what he was trying to communicate. Jack sighed and shook his head. "Go home, Mrs. Swift," he said evenly. "I'm staying with the kids."

Fanny looked longingly at the door, clearly wanting to leave, but stubbornness held her in place. She put her nose in the air, blew smoke and said, "I don't think so. We don't need you around here, Jack Tyler."

"Well, I need to be here," he said frankly. "Go home."

Fanny stubbed out her cigarette in a saucer. "Uh-uh."

"Go home, Granny," said an unexpected little voice.

Jack yanked his head around and saw Cody and Punk at the end of the hallway. Punk met his gaze squarely, then switched to her grandmother. Cody's mouth turned up in a smile so broad that it covered half his face, but Punk was doing the talking.

"Mister Tyler's gonna baby-sit us," she said firmly. "You just go on home. That way we won't have to stay in the bedroom so you can smoke."

"Dumb, stupid rule, anyway, if you ask me," Fanny muttered. Then she snatched up her purse, stuffed her cigarettes inside and hoisted the enormous gold and black leather bag onto one shoulder. She shook a finger at the kids. "You tell your mama not to call me again unless she really needs me. I got a life, you know."

"Yes, ma'am," Punk said absently, staring at Jack. He wanted to scoop her up and squeeze her, but something told him not to try it at this stage.

Fanny strode past him, teetering on her purple stilts. "I still think you're trouble for my girl," she said in a low voice as she made for the door. "That child never did know what was good for her."

Jack bit the inside of his cheek to forestall a reply to that, not knowing whether it would be a laugh or a curse. He shook his head as the door closed behind Fanny and smiled lamely at the kids. "I don't think your grandmother likes me."

Punk just looked at him, then walked over to slouch against the sofa. "Daddy says Fanny likes anyone and anything male."

"She's always saying how she's got more boyfriends than Mama," Cody added from the hallway.

Jack choked back one remark and chose another. "Maybe your mother just has better taste."

Cody considered that, then said, "And she works too much."

Jack nodded. "I won't argue with that, but she does it because she has to, you know, and I admire her for it. She's no quitter, your mom."

"Is that how come you like her?" Punk asked, eyes narrowed.

"That's one reason," Jack answered truthfully.

Punk seemed to find that acceptable. She climbed up onto the couch, sat down and folded her arms. He sensed that she was waiting for him to do or say something, but he didn't know what that might be. A screech from the vicinity of the bedroom saved him.

"Ya-a-ack!"

Jack chuckled. "Hold on, Davy, I'm coming."

He winked at Cody as he slipped by him in the hall. Cody winked back, smiling ear to ear, and gave him a quick thumbs up. Well, he'd done something right. Jack wasn't exactly sure what it was, but at the moment he didn't even care. It was enough that Cody was happy, that Davy couldn't wait to see him again, and that Punk, God love her crotchety little soul, had chosen him—actually chosen him—over someone else. It didn't even matter that the someone else had been Fanny Swift. For once, for the very first time, Punk had chosen him. He felt ten feet tall—and growing.

Heller worked her key in the lock and let herself into a living room lit only by the night-light plugged into an outlet in the far corner of the room. The television was off, and the house was quiet, almost unnaturally so. She frowned at the faint odor of tobacco smoke and wondered where Fanny was. Fanny seldom went to bed before daylight.

Laying her purse and extra clothing on the counter, she slipped off her shoes and quietly carried them into the hallway and to the door of the bedroom her children shared. She stooped and set the shoes on the floor then crept into the tiny room. All was as it should have been. Cody lay on his stomach in the top bunk, breathing through his mouth, his thick ash brown hair sticking out at odd angles, one bare leg peeking out from beneath the yellowed sheet. In the lower bunk, his sister slept on her back, both arms flung out, her light golden blond hair spread upon the pillow. Heller noted that her bangs needed a trim and made a mental note to get out the scissors tomorrow.

She turned to the crib in the corner. Davy lay face-down, arms and knees pulled in, his little rump in the air, a wet circle of drool near the corner of his mouth. He had kicked his covers down to the foot of the bed. Heller pulled the pink sheet—a leftover from Punk's infancy—up to his shoulders before tiptoeing from the room, picking up her shoes and moving on down the hall.

The bathroom was empty, the door open, which meant that Fanny was either sleeping in her bed or had committed the unpardonable sin of leaving her children alone, and Heller wouldn't have taken bets either way. Surely Fanny knew, however, that abandoning the children would ignite Heller's temper, and justifiably so. Prepared for the worst, Heller pushed open her bedroom door and flipped on the overhead light. The body in her bed did not belong to her mother.

"Jack!"

He rolled over onto his side and lifted an arm to shield his eyes from the sudden light.

"Hmm?"

He was too long for the bed, his stockinged feet hanging off the end. His sleek golden hair was mussed endearingly, the shadow of his beard on his jaws and chin quite dark in the harsh light. He yawned, rubbed both hands over his face and briefly groomed his mustache with his fingertips, then wedged his arm beneath his head, propping himself up on his elbow. He smiled sleepily.

"Hi, babe."

Heller could only gape and shake her head. "Jack, what are you doing here?"

His smile became a little sheepish. "Your couch is just too short," he said. "When I got sleepy, I knew that if I didn't move in here, I'd wind up packing ice on this knee again."

"I don't mean that," she said, moving into the room and dropping her shoes at the foot of the bed, right next to his, as it happened. "Well, I *do* mean that, but I also mean... Where's Mother?"

He grinned, actually pleased about something, so much so that he rolled onto his back, folded both arms beneath his head and crossed his ankles. Intrigued, she moved to the side of the bed so that she could look down into his face.

"What?" She was smiling herself.

"Punk sent her away," he said.

She blinked at him. "Punk?"

"Um-hm, right after I got here." The smile faded, and he pushed up onto his elbow again, his good knee cocking to provide him balance. "Didn't you know I wouldn't leave you in the lurch?"

"What do you mean?"

"I mean, I expected to stay with the kids myself at night. Mary Beth in the daytime, me at night."

She was gaping again. He sounded so... wounded. "Jack."

"Listen, if it's presumptuous of me, I mean, if I'm sticking my nose in where it doesn't belong, you just tell me, and I'll... I'll..." He sighed.

The dear man. She should have known he'd be here. She should've realized that the big heart he carried around inside that broad chest wouldn't allow him to walk away from someone else's problem. Or was it just her problems from which he couldn't walk away? God knew he'd been more help to her in a few short weeks than Carmody ever had during all the years of their marriage. In point of fact, he'd been as much husband to her as Carmody had, even though they weren't married and had never made love. She was standing there looking down at him, all rumpled and warm in her bed, trying to remember why she shouldn't lie down beside him and offer herself, body and soul. Never mind her heart. He already had that, blast him, and a lot of good it would do him, too. The poor man.

"You're bound and determined to complicate your life, aren't you?" she said, folding her arms.

He drew his brows together. "How so?"

"Jack," she said earnestly, "I don't have anything to offer you but trouble. I have three kids by an ex-husband who will never be anything but a headache. Just my upbringing and family background is enough to send most men running. I don't have a single viable asset, not even a bank account. Life's worn me to a nub, Jack, and I'm not even thirty! What do you want with a woman like me?"

A wistful kind of smile spread slowly across his face. He crooked a finger. "Come down here, and I'll show you."

She stared at him for a long time, but in the end she crawled up onto the bed and across him to sit astride his hips, her hands braced against his shoulders. He reached around and pulled the rubber band from her hair, allowing it to flow down her back in a silky cascade. He combed it forward with his fingers, framing her face.

"You're beautiful."

She tamped down the thrill that that produced and regarded him frankly. "Jack, I've had three children."

He grinned. "Acquired a few stretch marks, have you?"

"A few."

"I don't care."

Oh, how she wanted to believe that, but she shook her head. "You deserve better."

"Doesn't get any better than you," he told her. "You're beautiful from the inside out. You're strong and principled and dedicated. You have real character, Heller. Your children, too, young as they are."

She smiled at that. "Even Punk?"

"Especially Punk, because she's so like you."

Still smiling, she closed her eyes and whispered, "You're making me fall in love with you."

"God, I hope so!"

"Ah, Jack." She leaned forward on her knees and brought her mouth to his. He wrapped his arms around her and pulled her down on top of him, thrusting his hands into her hair at the back of her head. A liquid warmth spread through her body, and she became suddenly and excitedly aware of the length of hardness pressing against her belly.

His hand moved to her back, massaging and manipulating her shoulder blades so that her breasts rubbed against his chest, a friction so exquisite that it was akin to torture. She moaned into his mouth, her tongue following the sound to elicit one like it from him. His hands lifted away from her back and an instant later cupped the twin mounds of her buttocks, pressing her up and against him. Heller gasped at the fierceness of the sensation that flashed through her.

Suddenly Jack rolled onto his side, carrying her with him and thrusting a knee between her legs while one hand moved to knead her breast. Within moments she was lost, her head whirling in an attempt to keep up with the sensuous responses that he wrung from her body. Desperate to find an anchor, she closed a fist in the fabric of his shirt, twisting until it wrapped around her wrist.

"I *told* you."

The sound of her daughter's voice sliced neatly through the haze of passion. Heller froze, her desire cooled as effectively as if a pail of ice water had been dumped on her. In the same moment Jack groaned and flopped over onto his back.

"Punk," Cody scolded in a loud whisper, "look what you've done!"

Heller closed her eyes and waited for the embarrassment to come. Oddly enough it didn't, and after only an instant's reflection, she knew why. It was amazingly simple: she was right where she should be, and so was Jack. Smiling to herself, she struggled up onto her elbows and peered over Jack to the open doorway of her room.

"Little late for you guys to be up, isn't it?"

Cody fidgeted with the hem on one leg of the soft knit shorts he wore. "We, um, heard something."

Heller could imagine very well what they'd heard. She slid a look at Jack, who lifted one eyebrow and settled in to hear whatever might be said next, his arms folded behind his head. Before Heller could open her mouth, however, Punk lurched to the foot of the bed, her hands pressing flat into the mattress.

"Are you guys getting married?"

Cody gasped and made a grab for his sister's arm. "Punk! Shut up!"

She shrugged away. "No, I won't!"

"You're gonna scare him away before we even get him!"

Heller sat straight up on the bed. "Cody! Punk!"

Punk made an impatient motion, her gaze glued to Jack's face. "You scared?"

Heller smacked a hand against her chest, red now with the embarrassment that had failed to materialize before. "Punk, of all the things to say!"

To her surprise Jack began to chuckle. A hand came down on her knee as he shifted into a sitting position on the side of the bed. "It's okay, honey," he assured her. Then he leaned forward, his elbows on his knees and signaled for the kids to come closer.

Punk slid around the end of the bed to press herself against him, while Cody sprang forward from the door. Jack rubbed a big hand over the top of Cody's head, then curled a finger beneath Punk's chin, lifting her gaze to his.

"Nothing and nobody's scaring me off," he said evenly. "See, it's like this. I'm in love with your mother, but I don't think she's quite made up her mind about me, yet. When she does, we'll let you know. Okay?"

Cody nearly crowed, fanning his hands in a clapping motion while he danced from foot to foot. Jack smiled at him and got up. Punk tugged at his pants leg. Jack looked down at her.

"Does that mean you might be getting married?" she asked stubbornly.

Jack bent until his nose was nearly touching her nose. "That means," he said softly, "I'll let you know when I know." She bit her lip, then gave her head a sharp, satisfied nod.

Smiling, Jack stuffed his feet into his loafers, turned toward Heller and leaned across the bed for a quick kiss. "See you tomorrow, babe."

Just the look in his eyes warmed Heller immeasurably. She hugged her knees and smiled wanly, thrilled to the soles of her feet but yet uncertain. "Tomorrow," she agreed huskily.

Jack winked and walked out the door, giving each of the kids' heads a final pat on the way. Cody and Punk clambered up onto the bed, brimming with questions, questions to which she had no answers at the moment. She headed them off with a wave of her arms.

"You two belong in bed."

"But Mom—"

"In bed."

"Mo-ther," Cody whined.

She laid a finger across his mouth, then lifted a finger to point to the doorway. "Bed. Now."

Punk backed off the bed and grabbed her brother's hand, tugging. "Come on, Cody. Mom's tired. We can talk later."

Cody reluctantly let himself be pulled off the bed and out the door.

"I'll come tuck you in," Heller called. "Don't wake the baby."

She heard whispers and giggles in the hallway and knew perfectly well what they were talking about. She pictured herself and Jack as the kids must have seen them minutes earlier, and remembered sensation flooded her. *I'm in love with your mother... in love with your mother.*

"Oh, Jack," she whispered, "if only I was as good for you as you are for me."

And yet, he loved her.

She hugged that knowledge to herself and savored it for a long, heady moment. Only when Davy began to wail did she sigh and give up the memory, but she was smiling when she slipped from the bed.

Cody and Punk were shushing him and trying to get him to lie down when she got there, but he was having none of it. He looked to Heller, opening and closing one hand to indicate that he wanted something, and said, "Yack! Yack!" Heller hung her head, quietly laughing to herself.

How had that man become such a part of all their lives? She lifted Davy out of his bed and began patting him on the back, crooning softly until he laid his head upon her shoulder and drifted back to sleep. By the time she crawled back into bed, she was thoroughly exhausted. Yet, sleep did not come easily. Whenever she closed her eyes, she saw and felt Jack next to her.

I'm in love with your mother. I don't think she's quite made up her mind about me yet. I'm in love with your mother.

She sighed. If only it was as easy as telling him what was in her heart. If only she'd had different parents, if Carmody had just tried to support the family so she could go to school, if only she'd lived her life differently, she could go to Jack with a clean conscience and a full heart. But then she might have missed having her children. He might never even have come into her life. Still, what would people think if Jackson Tyler married the daughter of the notorious Swifts, not to mention the ex-wife of a bum like Carmody Moore? Jack was too honorable, too responsible to be saddled with her baggage.

Yet, her first thought when she woke in the morning was that she would see Jack when she got home from work. She rose from bed impatient for the day to end. So, naturally every moment seemed to drag on eternally. By the time she left for work, she was seething with frustration, and the day did not get better. Sales at the store were unusually slow; she spent long stretches of time by herself, trying not to hope that Jack would come in or be disappointed when he didn't.

Only by sheer dint of will did she refrain from calling in to beg off her shift at the nursing home, but her impatience was so evident that her supervisor feared she was becoming ill and insisted that she take off an hour early. Heller didn't argue with her, even though she knew that the only thing wrong with her was that Jack Tyler had become entirely too necessary to her sense of well-being.

When she climbed the steps to her front door and let herself inside, it was to find Jack wide awake in the living room and playing a video game. A video game? Taking a closer look, she realized that it wasn't even her television with the lit-up screen.

He shot her a quick smile, put down the controller and got up to welcome her with a kiss. Afterward, she stood in the circle of his arms, her cheek laid over his heart, so that she felt the pulsing in his chest.

"You're home early," he said.

"My supervisor insisted. I wasn't feeling much like myself tonight."

He drew back slightly and curved his hand beneath her chin, lifting her face to his. "Something wrong, sweetheart?"

She shook her head, smiling. God help her, nothing could be wrong when he held her like this. "I'm just tired," she whispered, going up on tiptoe and looping her arms around his neck.

His hands moved to her sides, holding her lightly just above the waist. "Can I assume that you didn't sleep any better than I did last night?"

She just leaned against his chest and stared up at him. "Oh, Jack, what are we going to do?"

His arms came around her, and he tucked her head beneath his chin. "Love each other," he replied softly. "Make our family whole."

Our family. Emotion clogged Heller's throat. "If only I could be sure—"

He squeezed her tightly. "I understand. You have reason to be careful, so do I for that matter."

"Do you?"

He framed her face with his hands and tilted her head back. "You're not the only one who made a bad first marriage."

She smiled wanly. "Did she cheat on you, then?"

He shrugged. "I doubt it. We just wanted different things. She wanted to be married to a pro football player. I wanted to do something really important with my life, and I wanted to do it with children. She didn't understand that. She didn't want children of her own, and she didn't understand why I did."

"Carmody didn't want Davy," she whispered, surprised at the pain it still caused her.

Jack lifted an eyebrow. "Well, we know what kind of a fool Carmody is," he told her wryly.

She chuckled at that, and then she pulled back. "Now about this video game..."

Jack sighed dramatically and lifted his hands in a gesture of helplessness. "A guy's got to have something to do in the wee hours. Besides, the kids got a big kick out of it."

"No doubt," she commented dryly. "And the television?"

Jack scratched an ear. "Well, um, I couldn't figure out how to hook it up to your old set, which I put in your bedroom, by the way."

"Did you?" She tried to sound stern and failed.

Jack grinned at her. "I figured the kids could watch different channels if they wanted to."

"And what about you?"

"Oh, I don't watch much TV when I'm at the apartment, and if I wanted to, there's one in my bedroom."

"You're pretty sneaky, aren't you?"

He adopted an expression of confused innocence. "Me?"

Heller shook her head, fighting a smile. "What am I going to do with you?"

His hands closed around her arms, and he pulled her to him. "Shall I demonstrate?"

Heller closed her eyes and wrapped her arms around his waist. She knew that she should send him home, but it was beyond her. She made a sudden decision. It wouldn't hurt anything if they just rolled along as they were for a few weeks. The tough decisions could be put off for a bit longer, and in the meantime, she could have this much of him. She smiled and whispered, "Yes, please."

As expected, he did a very thorough job of it.

Chapter Ten

He didn't get up off the couch when she let herself into the trailer. It had become something of a ritual with them. He always stood to welcome her home by taking her in his arms and kissing her crazy. She felt dearly loved when he did that and very much a lady. So it struck her as odd when he didn't get up, and she had to admit to a good bit of disappointment. Still, it was a small thing, too small to worry about, and the disappointment abated when he put his head back, smiled as if delighted to see her, and lifted his arms.

She went to his side, the arm of the sofa between them, and dropped a kiss on his mouth. He coiled his arms around her and pulled her onto his lap, proceeding to scramble her brains with his toe-curling kisses. When they either had to stop or take it another step forward, he stopped and moved on to phase two of the nightly ritual.

"How was your day?"

Smiling, she snuggled against him. Did a dearer, more

trustworthy man exist in this world? "Same-old same-old," she said. "What about yours?"

He rubbed a hand up and down her back. "We started looking at our enrollment needs today. We're probably going to have to do some classroom shuffling to get everyone situated. Lots of new students are coming in, especially in the lower grades."

"Do we have room for them all?"

"So far. It's just a matter of organization. If this trend keeps up, though, we're going to have to look into building some additional space."

"Will that be your responsibility?"

"In a way. I'd be working with the superintendent and the school board to determine needs. Oh, you ought to know that I told Brent that I might be getting married."

She sat up straight, shocked. "Jack!"

"Well, he has a right to know. He knows you, by the way."

A feeling of dread descended. "And?"

Jack smiled and pulled the rubber band from her hair, spreading it across her shoulders. "He started here as a middle-school science teacher, you know."

"He remembers me from middle school?"

Jack nodded. "He remembers you well. He says you were one of the most promising students he's ever had, despite the lack of encouragement from home. He also says that you were more mature than the other kids, and understandably so. He was sad but not surprised when he heard that you'd dropped out of school to get married. Now he's delighted to hear that you've found someone who will treat you as you deserve to be treated. He wished us well and suggested that we plan an evening with him and his wife."

It took a moment for all that to sink in. When it did, she wasn't sure that she could trust it. "He couldn't have said that. Could he?"

Jack sighed and brushed the backs of his fingers across her cheek. "Sweetheart, when are you going to admit that you've been worrying about nothing?"

She looked at him in surprise. "What do you mean *worrying?*"

He chuckled. "I know you better than you think. You're happy with me. You won't make love with me until we're married, but you want to." He leaned forward and smacked a kiss on her lips, then leaned back again, smiling, and added, "Badly."

She couldn't deny it. Her body was burning even now, but she had to think of more than her desires. She wouldn't risk becoming pregnant. She wouldn't trap him that way, and she wouldn't expose her children to the scandal. Moreover, she would not dishonor herself by giving herself to any man outside of marriage; she'd be just like Carmody's numerous women if she did, and she would never, ever be that. She took a deep breath. "You wouldn't marry me just to sleep with me, would you, Jack?"

He studied her face as if trying to determine if she was serious. Deciding that she was, he answered her seriously. "Heller, I don't want to *sleep* with you at all. I want to make love to you in every sense of the word, and I want to marry you because I want to know that you're mine. I want to take care of you and the kids. I want you not to work yourself to death and enjoy life for a change."

Her eyes filled. Her bottom lip trembled. She looped her arms around his neck. "Oh, Jack, if only I could know that marrying you was the right thing to do."

"It's the right thing for me," he said, pulling her close, "and I honestly believe that it's the right thing for you and the kids. But you have to make up your own mind."

"I know," she whispered, "and I will, but whatever happens, I need you to remember something."

"What's that?"

"I love you, Jack."

He closed his eyes and let out a long, satisfied breath, a slow smile spreading across his face. "I love you, too," he said, a hand clamping onto her nape to pull her forward for his kiss.

It wasn't long before sitting on the couch and necking like teenagers wasn't enough, but for once Jack was not willing to stop. He leaned sideways, lowering her back to the cushions, and shifted in order to cover her body with his. Suddenly, he jerked back, air hissing through his teeth. Heller sprang up into a sitting position.

"Jack, what's wrong?"

"It's this darn knee," he gritted out, clutching his leg. Heller scrambled off the couch and snapped on the overhead light. What she saw chilled her to the bone. The knee had swollen so large that it had filled his jeans leg to the point of bursting.

"Sweet heavens! How did this happen?"

Jack grimaced. "It was all my fault. I was playing horse and rider with the kids." He grinned crookedly. "I was the horse."

"Jack!" she scolded.

He shrugged sheepishly. "It's a guy thing. Women dream of rocking their babies. Men see themselves galloping around on hands and knees with a giggling kid on their backs."

She couldn't help grinning at the spectacle *that* must have made. No doubt the children had been delighted. Yet she felt she had to be stern. He had hurt himself, after all! "A man as intelligent as you ought to be able to take care of himself," she said stiltedly. "Now take your pants off."

Both eyebrows shot up. *"What?"*

She realized what she'd said and blushed bright red. "I— I mean..." But this was for him, for his well-being. She pushed her shoulders back. "That leg is so swollen that your jeans are cutting off the circulation, and that has to make it hurt even worse. Now, I'm going to make you an ice pack, and I expect you to drop those jeans before I get back."

He grinned. "Yes, ma'am." Obediently he slid to the edge of the seat, leaned back and reached for his zipper. Heller whirled away and quickly marched into the kitchen, where she broke out ice cubes and wrapped them in kitchen toweling. She used a rolling pin to crush them into a more manageable mass, then steeled herself and returned to the living room. Jack was sitting with one of her tattered throw pillows covering his lap, his pants around his ankles.

"Have you taken anything for that?" she asked, and he nodded. She went down on her knees in front of him and gingerly placed the ice pack. He flinched but made no sound. She bit her lip, genuinely concerned. "I think you should call the doctor about this."

"I'll call tomorrow if it's still this bad," he promised.

She nodded, knowing that he would keep his word. "I wish there was something else we could do now."

He smoothed a hand over her hair. "You've already done more than you know," he said softly.

Smiling, she leaned into his good leg and stretched upward, searching for his mouth. He leaned forward to accommodate her, but their lips had barely met when the door burst open and Carmody stumbled inside.

"Heller!" he called much too loudly, his gaze ricocheting around the room and quickly finding her. He swayed and stumbled backward, lip curling in a sneer. "Well, looky here. Li'l Mizz Perfec' doin' a job on Misher Clean!" He put his head back and laughed, nearly toppling over in the process.

Heller shot straight to her feet. He was drunk as a skunk and twice as mean, but she would not let this insult pass. "How dare you! You have no right to be in my house! And for your information, he's injured his knee. I was putting an ice pack on it."

Carmody snickered and leaned toward Jack, wobbling somewhat. "Is big ol' Jack hurt 'isse'f? Wal, I bet li'l Heller can make it real good."

"You nasty-minded snake!" Heller spat. "Don't you dare talk to him like that!" Meanwhile Jack shook his head, sighed and got to his feet, pulling up his jeans. Heller's eyes widened. She knew exactly what he was going to do, and she was suddenly frightened for him. "Jack, darling, don't do anything you'll regret. He's not worth it, Jack, and...and you're already hurt!"

Carmody didn't have sense enough to know what was coming. He swayed and looped an arm around Heller's shoulder to steady himself, taunting, "Whazza matter, Jack? I shpoil your party? And I bet it took all dish time to get 'er dish far, didn' it? She's a cold li'l bi—"

"That's it," Jack said calmly, cutting off the other man with a hand clamped around his throat. "Time you figured out that you're not welcome here unless invited first." Without further preamble, Jack lifted Carmody off the floor and tossed him, literally, head-first out the door.

Heller gasped as Carmody flew over the stoop and landed with an "oof" on the ground. Jack calmly stepped out and descended the stairs, limping far less than Heller expected. She knew then that he was livid, despite the outer calm. She ran after him, arriving just as he picked Carmody up out of the dust by his shirt front.

"Now then," he said, his voice rumbling low in his chest, "do not—and I repeat do *not*—ever again just open the door and walk into Heller's house."

"You can't tell me what to do!" Carmody snarled, wiping dirt from his eye with the back of his hand.

"Oh, but I can," Jack replied. "It's really very simple. I'm in. You're out. And from now on you'll either behave like a gentleman in Heller's presence or you'll answer to me. Do you understand?"

"Understand this!" Carmody snarled. Heller screamed as his foot swung out and connected with Jack's swollen knee.

Jack clamped his jaws together, keeping his own scream behind his grinding teeth. Then he shook himself and smiled coldly into Carmody's face. "I see that you need further instruction. Lesson number one, having a weakness and being weak are two different things. Let me demonstrate." So saying, he doubled up his fist and drove it into Carmody's abdomen.

Carmody gasped and doubled over, but as he straightened up, he kicked again at Jack's knee. Jack caught his foot and flipped him onto his back like so many rags in a bundle. He had just picked up Carmody again, obviously intending another "demonstration," when Punk hurled herself at him, fists flailing.

"Let go my dad! Let go my dad!"

Shocked, Heller felt a bump against her side and looked down to find Cody rubbing his fists against his eyes sleepily. "What's happening?" he croaked. "Somebody screamed."

Heller groaned and threw her arms around him, calling to her daughter to stop. "It's his own fault. He burst in drunk and insulted Jack and me."

"I don't care!" Punk sobbed. "He's my daddy!"

Jack had frozen, but he suddenly released Carmody and stepped back. "She's right," he said, pushing a hand through his hair.

Carmody stumbled and fell.

"Daddy!"

He pushed himself up to his feet, growling, "Shtop that screeshing!" He wiped a hand over his face, weaving side to side, and grumbled, "Damn kids're always screeshing." With that he stumbled off into the darkness.

Punk stood where she was, her little face ashen and strained, and then she crumbled into sobs. Heller immediately started forward, hugging Cody to her side. "Oh, Punk, don't. I'm sure he didn't mean it. He's just too drunk to know what he's saying."

To her surprise, Jack waved her back. Then he bent and scooped her little girl into his arms. Limping badly now, he carried her to the steps and sat down. "I'm sorry, honey," he said, pushing back her hair and wiping tears from her face. "I shouldn't have let him make me mad. Your mom's right, he was too drunk to know what he was doing. I had no business roughing him up."

Punk sniffed and astounded Heller by cuddling up in his lap. "My dad's pretty much no good," she said in a trembling voice.

Jack seemed to think that over, then he said, "That may be true, but he's still you're father, and sometimes it can be nice being his little girl. Try to concentrate on those times, okay?"

Punk slowly nodded her head. Looking up into his face, she asked, "What's it like to be your little girl?"

Jack shrugged. "I don't know because I don't have a little girl of my own. I can tell you this, though, I wouldn't name her Punk like she was some street tough looking for a fight."

"It's not my real name, you know," she said wistfully.

Jack smiled gently. "I figured. Why don't you tell me your real name? Maybe we can find something else to call you."

She sat up straight and folded her hands in her lap primly, saying, "It's Rosalie Evangeline."

"That's a beautiful name!" Jack exclaimed.

She leaned against his chest and frowned. "But it's too long!" she insisted.

Jack tucked her comfortably into the crook of his arm, saying, "Well, maybe we can shorten it up some. How about Rosie?"

Punk screwed up her face.

"No? Okay, then what about..." He smiled as inspiration struck. "Angel. Short for Evangeline."

Her face took on a look of awe. "Angel," she breathed.

Jack grinned. "You like that? Then from now on, you're Angel to me."

She sighed, sounding for all the world like a girl smitten with a new hero. Then suddenly she snapped around and looked directly at her mother. "You better marry this guy quick, Mom."

Heller's mouth fell open. Cody jumped up and down, clapping his hands and laughing. Jack hugged "Angel" and grinned at Heller. "Yeah, Mom," he agreed, *"quick."*

Heller had to close her mouth before she could speak. "After what happened here tonight," she said in wonder, "you still want to marry me?"

Jack cocked his head. "Why wouldn't I? I still love you."

Heller lifted a hand to cover her pounding heart, too touched to speak.

Jack calmly set Angel on her feet and motioned to Cody. Cody came forward eagerly, pulling his mother along with him. "Son, take your sister into the house." His eyes were on Heller. He stretched out his leg, testing it, grimaced and reached for her hand in the same instant that Cody moved to grasp his sister by her shoulders and ease her away. Jack pulled Heller down onto his lap and gathered her close.

"When are you going to understand?" he said. "I love you, and nothing's going to change that."

She framed his face with her hands. "I just don't want to hurt you."

"Then marry me," he said, "because if you don't I will be hurt."

"Jack."

"Heller, I'm never going to be happy without you. I can't even go back to the way I was before I met you, and I think that you and the children need me. Anyway, I hope you do because I need you to."

Heller sighed, giving in. She was too tired to fight him anymore. She just didn't have the heart for it. "You know we do," she whispered.

Smiling, he pulled her head down onto his shoulder and kissed her. Slowly she lifted her arm and slid it around his neck, at the same time letting go of all her worries. She would make him the best wife possible, she vowed silently. She had no doubt that he would be the finest husband in all the world. He deepened the kiss, sliding his tongue into her mouth and his hand up her side and around to cup her breast. A giggle alerted them both. Jack dropped his hand as Heller jerked upright. They both turned to find Cody and Angel grinning at them.

Heller swallowed a gasp. "I heard Jack tell you to go inside."

"It's well past your bedtime," he said in his best principal's voice.

"Now go," Heller added.

The children ran beside them and up the steps, giggling, but on the stoop they paused and looked at one another. Cody stepped forward, put his hands on Jack's shoulders and leaned over to give his mother a kiss, veering off at the last moment to smack in Jack's ear. Surprised, Jack laughed and jerked his head around, causing Angel's kiss to land between his eye and the bridge of his nose. Giggling, she ran into the house, a beaming Cody right behind her. Jack chuckled and called out, "Don't wake the baby." Shaking his head, he said to Heller, "I love them, too, you know."

She nodded, smiling happily. "I know."

He pulled her head down onto his shoulder again. "Listen, I've been thinking. I've got enough money in the bank to buy us a house, just pay for it outright. That way, everyone could have his or her own bedroom, and you wouldn't have to work."

"Not work!" Heller exclaimed. "Do you mean it?"

Jack smiled. "Sure, why not? Wouldn't you like to stay home with the kids?"

"Oh, Jack, I'd love it! They're growing up so fast. It's like I'm missing everything."

"Well, that's decided then. Unless you'd rather go to college."

"College!" She sat bolt upright. "How do you know about that?"

"About you wanting to go? Your mother told me."

Heller frowned. "I just bet she did."

"All right, so she isn't in favor of it. That doesn't mean you can't go if you want to."

Heller stared at him. For the longest time she'd wanted to go to college, knowing it was the only way to ensure a better life for her children. She hadn't counted on Jackson Tyler. How could she have? She trailed her fingertips over his face. "I think I'd rather have another baby first," she told him softly.

He looked for a moment as if he might cry. Then he closed his eyes and put his forehead to hers. "Oh, Heller, thank you! I love you so much!"

"I love you, too," she said, putting her arms around him and laughing happily while he kissed her ear and her throat and her collarbone.

Suddenly he lifted his head. "I won't love our baby any more than I love our other kids. You know that, don't you?"

She nodded. "Yes, I know that."

He squeezed her so tightly she thought her ribs would break. Then his mouth was on hers and his hand was sliding beneath her shirt.

Suddenly a wail filled the air. Groaning, they pulled apart, got up, and climbed the stairs side by side. Jack was chuckling before they got through the living room. "I think I'm going to put a lock on our bedroom door," he announced.

Heller laughed. "Think it'll help?"

"Maybe a nanny," he muttered.

Heller saw the light beneath the bedroom door and shook her head. "More like a warden."

He straightened his face with some effort and thrust the door open. The two older kids were standing beside Davy's bed, trying to pat him into silence. Davy was on his feet, howling like a banshee, not a tear in his eyes. Jack looked at the older two and said, "I thought you were going to try not to wake him."

"We did," Cody said, but Angel leaned forward and whispered in Davy's ear, her hand cupped around her mouth. The wail shut off abruptly. Suddenly Davy turned and hurled himself at the foot of the crib, his arms flung out in a bid to be picked up. "Daddy!" he cried.

Jack's mouth fell open. His gaze fastened on Angel even as he absently plucked Davy from his bed. "Did you tell him to call me that?"

She shrugged. "Carmody doesn't pay him any attention, anyway. He wasn't even around when he got borned."

Jack shot a look at Heller. His eyes had a liquid shine to them. He cupped Davy's head in his big hand and kissed his forehead.

"Can we pick out the new house?" Angel asked tellingly.

Jack laughed. "We'll pick it out together."

"I hope the new baby's a girl," she said. "Then it'd be even."

"Baby!" Heller and Jack exclaimed in unison.

"Well, you said you were going to have another baby," Cody explained defensively.

"Not for a long while yet," Heller said briskly.

"Yeah," Jack said, his voice choked with laughter. "We have to get married first. Then it'll take at least nine months."

"At least," Heller reiterated. Then she looked at Jack and they both burst out laughing. Davy laughed, too, though it was obvious he didn't have the slightest clue about what was funny.

Jack caught his breath, wiped his eyes and pulled Heller to him, one arm about her shoulders, the other holding Davy. She slid her arms around his waist. "Okay," Jack said, "it's obvious no one's feeling particularly sleepy right now, so we might as well talk this over and set a date, an early one."

The older two hurrahed and bounced up onto the bottom bunk. Davy clapped his hands together, his wiggling brows betraying his confusion. Jack chuckled and walked over to the bed. Keeping one arm around Davy, he turned around, sat down and hunched over, easing himself beneath the upper bunk to lean on one elbow, then waved Heller over to join them. She didn't have nearly so much trouble fitting between the beds as he did. She just sat down on the edge of the bunk and scooted back so that she was nestled in the curve of his body. Davy grabbed a handful of her hair and pulled himself into her lap.

Jack pretended to glare at him. "Traitor."

Davy giggled, certain this was all in fun, too. Heller hugged him and said to Jack, "Now you know how it feels."

He chucked her under the chin, smiling. Angel threw herself down on her stomach, head supported by her fists and declared, "I want to be a bride girl."

"You mean a flower girl," Heller said, leaning forward to tap her on the end of the nose. Everyone laughed.

In the silence that followed, Cody said, "I think putting up that ad was the smartest thing I ever did!"

Jack reached out to ruffle his hair, his eyes finding Heller's. "And the smartest thing I ever did was answer it."

Heller smiled, feeling the warmth of his gaze flow over her. "I think you're right," she said, her voice sounding breathless and husky. "I think we ought to set an early date."

Jack's hand curled around hers where it lay against the bed.

They laughed and made plans until the dawn peeked over the horizon, brightening the room. Davy had long ago fallen asleep on Heller's shoulder, and Cody was yawning wide enough to turn himself inside out. Angel crawled up to the head of the bed and laid down upon the pillow, her hand patting Jack's shoulder.

Chuckling to himself, he slid out onto the floor and straightened, groaning with stiff muscles and various cricks. Heller pushed up beside him, swaying with exhaustion but smiling. He ushered her over to the crib and helped her lower Davy into it. She covered him while Jack went to give Cody a boost onto the top bunk and help him pull up his covers. Heller covered Angel, and together she and Jack walked out into the hall. He pulled the door closed and directed her toward her own bedroom, his hand resting in the small of her back.

"Heavens, I'm tired," she said, covering a yawn with her hand.

"Me, too, babe." He opened the door and they went in together. "We'll grab a couple hours of sleep then get busy. We've got a lot to do."

Heller smiled and plopped down on the bed. Kicking off her shoes, she crawled over into the middle of the bed and stretched out. Jack followed, leaving his shoes beside hers. He slid an arm beneath her head and rolled to his side, curving his other arm possessively about her waist. She snuggled against his big body, sighed and closed her eyes.

"I don't think I told you," he said, "I have a king-size bed."

"Ah," Heller sighed, and together they drifted off to sleep.

Jack was dreaming of having Heller in that big bed of his when a loud noise jerked him awake. He rolled over to find Fanny Swift waving a smoking cigarette. "You little idiot!" she screamed. "I told you he was only after sex!"

Heller opened her eyes a crack and moaned. "Mother, what are you doing here?"

"Carmody told me what he walked in on last night!" she huffed.

Jack sucked in a breath of air in an attempt to clear his head, coughed and waved away the cigarette smoke. "Put that thing out!"

"Don't get smart with me, lying there in my daughter's bed!"

Jack surged up onto one elbow. "For your information," he said, "your daughter won't make love with me until we're married. That's been her position all along."

"Married!" Fanny gasped.

"That's right, married," Jack said smartly. "If you'd open your eyes, you'd see that we were sleeping fully clothed on top of the covers. Now get out of here. I won't have you walking in anytime you please, upsetting my family."

"*Your* family!"

"Yes, *his* family," Heller said, lifting up onto her elbow next to Jack. "He loves us and takes care of us," she added "which is more than Carmody has ever done."

"But Carmody fathered your children!" Fanny gasped her bright orange lipstick clashing with her orange body suit.

"No, he didn't," Heller said stubbornly. "He planted them. Jack fathers them."

Fanny looked as if she couldn't believe what she wa hearing. The cigarette between her fingers, meanwhile, ha burned down to the filter. Suddenly she yelped, dropped th glowing butt onto the floor and stomped it out with he platform sandals.

"Mother!" Heller lurched up into a sitting position.

"It's all right," Jack said soothingly, looking over th edge of the bed. "It's out. There's a spot on the floor, bu we'll be moving soon, anyway."

"Moving!" Fanny bleated.

"Yes, moving," Heller said, folding her legs into a pre zel shape. "We're going to buy a house."

Fanny was clearly astounded. "A house?"

"With four bedrooms," Heller informed her smugl "and new living room furniture, a dining suite, and a kin size bed."

Fanny scoffed. "Yeah, right, and when are you going t manage that...in time for the kids to go off on their own?'

"Today, hopefully," Jack said, crossing his ankles wit admirable nonchalance. "Since we're paying cash we won have to worry about things like credit checks and loan a provals."

"C-c-cash!"

It was all Jack could do not to laugh. She looked so con ical standing there in that ridiculous outfit, her bleached ha fluffed out around a bright green headband, orange mouth gaping.

"It has to be soon," Heller explained. "We're getting married in five days."

"Four," Jack corrected her.

She smiled at him. "Four."

Fanny's legs seemed to collapse. She plopped onto the floor in shock. "You're serious!"

Jack rolled onto his side, folding an arm beneath his head and groping with the other for Heller's hand. He found it, laid it on his hip and covered it with his own. "I told you once before," he said, looking down at Fanny, "you underestimate your daughter. Any man would be glad to make her his wife. I'm just the lucky one who's going to do it."

Fanny switched her incredulous gaze to Heller. "What about Carmody?"

Heller shrugged. "What about him? He has no say in my life anymore."

"No one's saying that he can't see the kids," Jack said. "They're his children, after all. However, he'll call and make arrangements first, or he'll be turned away at the door. Do us all a favor and make sure he understands that. He was too drunk last night to get it, and in future, *that* had better not happen again, either."

"That goes for you, too, Mother," Heller said firmly. "From now on you'll call first, and I don't want to smell liquor on your breath when you get here."

"And no smoking around the kids," Jack added, "or me."

"Or me," Heller echoed.

Fanny looked around as if expecting rescue, then she shook her head and threw up her hands. Sighing, she got to her feet, a process Jack hoped never to see repeated. "You two are just alike," she said, "stick-in-the-muds, no fun at all."

Jack smiled and rolled onto his back, looking at Heller. "Guess us stick-in-the-muds just belong together."

Heller nodded and stretched out beside him on her belly, her arms sliding over his chest. "I don't know about us not having any fun, though. I suspect we've got lots of good times ahead of us."

Jack chuckled and pulled her up onto his chest, his arms holding her there. "Lots of good times," he promised.

"I love you," Heller said softly.

"I'm a lucky man," he told her, "even if it's just half as much as I love you."

She stretched upward to brush her mouth against his.

"Close the door behind you, Fanny," he said, his eyes promising Heller much more than fun. They would have joy. It was their destiny, a destiny drawn, happily, in crayon

*   *   *   *   *

He's able to change a diaper in three seconds flat.
And melt an unsuspecting heart even quicker.
But changing his mind about marriage might take some doing!
He's more than a man...
He's a **FABULOUS FATHER!**

****

Cuddle up this winter with these handsome hunks:

October:
INTRODUCING DADDY by Alaina Hawthorne (RS#1180)
He just discovered his soon-to-be ex-wife "forgot" to
tell him he's a daddy!

November:
DESPERATELY SEEKING DADDY by Arlene James (RS#1186)
Three little kids advertise for a father—and a husband for
their beautiful single mom....

December:
MERRY CHRISTMAS, DADDY by Susan Meier (RS#1192)
A bachelor fumbles with rattles and baby pins—and his love for
a woman—all in time for Christmas!

January:
MAD FOR THE DAD by Terry Essig (RS#1198)
Overwhelmed by his new daddy responsibilities, he needs a
little help from his pretty neighbor....

***

Celebrate fatherhood—and love!—every month.
FABULOUS FATHERS...only in *Silhouette* ROMANCE™

The Calhoun Saga continues...

in November
New York Times bestselling author

NORA ROBERTS

takes us back to the Towers and introduces us to
the newest addition to the Calhoun household,
sister-in-law Megan O'Riley in

MEGAN'S MATE
(Intimate Moments #745)

And in December
look in retail stores for the special collectors'
trade-size edition of

THE
Calhoun
Women

containing all four fabulous Calhoun series books:
COURTING CATHERINE,
A MAN FOR AMANDA, FOR THE LOVE OF LILAH
and *SUZANNA'S SURRENDER.*
Available wherever books are sold.

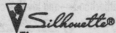

FORTUNE'S Children™

Bestselling Author
LINDA TURNER

Continues the twelve-book series—FORTUNE'S CHILDREN—
in **November 1996** with Book Five

THE WOLF AND THE DOVE

Adventurous pilot Rachel Fortune and traditional Native American
doctor Luke Greywolf set sparks off each other the minute they met.
But widower Luke was tormented by guilt and vowed never to love
again. Could tempting Rachel heal Luke's wounded heart so they
could share a future of happily ever after?

MEET THE FORTUNES—a family whose legacy is greater than riches.
Because where there's a will…there's a *wedding!*

A CASTING CALL TO
ALL FORTUNE'S CHILDREN FANS!
If you are truly fortunate,
you may win a trip to
Los Angeles to audition for
Wheel of Fortune®. Look for
details in all retail Fortune's Children titles!

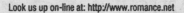

Look us up on-line at: http://www.romance.net   FC-5-C

The collection of the year!
NEW YORK TIMES BESTSELLING AUTHORS

Linda Lael Miller
Wild About Harry

Janet Dailey
Sweet Promise

Elizabeth Lowell
Reckless Love

Penny Jordan
Love's Choices

and featuring
Nora Roberts
The Calhoun Women

This special trade-size edition features four of the wildly
popular titles in the Calhoun miniseries together in
one volume—a true collector's item!

Pick up these great authors and a chance to win
a weekend for two in New York City at the
Marriott Marquis Hotel on Broadway! We'll pay
for your flight, your hotel—even a Broadway show!

Available in December at your favorite retail outlet.

NEW YORK
Marriott.
MARQUIS

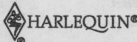 

NYT1296-R

This holiday season,
Linda Varner brings three very special couples

HOME
FOR THE HOLIDAYS

where they discover the joy of love and family—
and the wonder of wedded bliss.

❄❄❄❄❄❄❄❄❄❄❄❄❄❄❄❄❄❄❄❄❄❄❄❄❄

WON'T YOU BE MY HUSBAND?—Lauren West and
Nick Gatewood never expected their family and friends to get
word of their temporary engagement and nonintended nuptials. Or
to find themselves falling in love with each other. Is that a *real*
wedding they're planning over Thanksgiving dinner?
(SR#1188, 11/96)

MISTLETOE BRIDE—There was plenty of room at Dani Sellica's
Colorado ranch for stranded holiday guests Ryan Given and his
young son. Until the mistletoe incident! Christmas morning brought
presents from ol' Saint Nick…but would it also bring wedding bells?
(SR#1193, 12/96)

NEW YEAR'S WIFE—Eight years after Tyler Jordan and
Julie McCrae shared a passionate kiss at the stroke of midnight,
Tyler is back and Julie is certain he doesn't fit into her plans for
wedded bliss. But does his plan to prove her wrong include a lifetime
of New Year's kisses? (SR#1200, 1/97)

Add a double dash of romance to your
festivities this holiday season
with two great stories in

Christmas
Celebration

Featuring full-length stories by bestselling authors

Kasey Michaels
Anne McAllister

These heartwarming stories of love triumphing
against the odds are sure to add some extra
Christmas cheer to your holiday season. And this
distinctive collection features **two full-length novels,**
making it the perfect gift at great value—for
yourself or a friend!

Available this December at your favorite retail outlet.

V *Silhouette*®
™
...where passion lives.

Concluding in November from Silhouette books...

This exciting new cross-line continuity series unites five of your favorite authors as they weave five connected novels about love, marriage—and Daddy's unexpected need for a baby carriage!

You fell in love with the wonderful characters in:

THE BABY NOTION by Dixie Browning (Desire 7/96)

BABY IN A BASKET by Helen R. Myers
(Romance 8/96)

MARRIED...WITH TWINS! by Jennifer Mikels
(Special Edition 9/96)

HOW TO HOOK A HUSBAND (AND A BABY)
by Carolyn Zane (Yours Truly 10/96)

And now all of your questions will finally be answered in

DISCOVERED: DADDY
by Marilyn Pappano (Intimate Moments 11/96)

Everybody is still wondering...who's the father of prim and proper Faith Harper's baby? But Faith isn't letting anyone in on her secret—not until she informs the daddy-to-be. Trouble is, *he* doesn't seem to remember her....

Don't miss the exciting conclusion of
DADDY KNOWS LAST...only in Silhouette books!